GAP-TOOTHED GIRL

THE STORY OF A LITTLE RUNAWAY WITH INDESTRUCTIBLE INTEGRITY

BY RAY HARVEY

To Angelina,
who asked about my
literature. May all your
dreams come true.

Ray

PEARL BUTTON PRESS

Gap-Toothed Girl

Copyright © 2018 by Ray Harvey

First published September 2018 by Pearl Button Press

Harvey, Ray

Gap-Toothed Girl

p. cm.

ISBN 978-0-9823979-8-5

PART I

Ballerina Bianca Passarge, of Hamburg, June 1958

TOURNAMENT NIGHT in a sweltering Las Vegas stadium, and the girl with the gap-toothed smile stood bleeding in her ballet slippers. The sodium lights of the arena lay upcast on the low-hanging sky above. An electrical charge hummed through the air: a crackling undercurrent that came neither from the lights nor from the distant heat lightning, but from the galvanized excitement of the crowd.

Before her, some twenty feet away and elevated four feet off the ground, there stretched a long green balance beam, atop which, at the southernmost end, stood eight empty whiskey bottles. The bottles were perfectly upright and in single file. A small springboard crouched in front.

High above her floated a long banner which said, in shimmering red letters:

A CONTEST OF MOTION

She closed her eyes and inhaled. The air was dry. She stood alone upon the stage. She was dusky-limbed, Lakota. She held her breath a moment and then she released it.

When she opened her eyes, her gaze settled on the objects before her: the springboard, the balance beam, the whiskey bottles. The heat hung heavy. A rill of sweat slid between her breasts. She didn't see the tiny camera-flash explosions igniting everywhere around her from within the darkness of the stadium. She forgot that there were thousands of eyes fixed upon her. She forgot also the pain in her toes and was unaware of the blood leaking like ink across the entire top part of her slipper.

Offstage in the shadows, a lanky youth in a baseball cap gave a thumbs-up, but it wasn't directed toward her.

A man with a microphone emerged on stage. He was thin and well-dressed and darkly complexioned.

A hush came over the crowd. The man held the microphone to his mouth. His voice came booming through the speakers with great clarity.

"Ladies and gentlemen," he said, "ladies and gentleman. May I have your attention, please. Thank you. We are finally at the end of the night, and — my Lord — what a night it's been. What a competition."

The crowd erupted.

"We have seen — excuse me, please — we have seen tonight some of the very best dancers in the world, and I'm sure you know this is not an exaggeration. We have only one more to go. Did we save the best for last? Need I remind you that there's fifty *thousand* dollars at stake here?"

He paused.

"Now," he said, "now, then. Do you see this young woman up on the stage with me? I'm told she's about to do something that only one other person in human history is known to have done, and that was Ms. Bianca Passarge, of Hamburg, Germany, in 1958 — except Ms. Passarge, I am told, was not mounting a balance beam when she did her routine. Can this little girl — all 115 pounds of her — I say, can she do it? Can she steal the money from these big city boys and girls, the Bronx break dancers and West Coast B-Boys and all the others who have astounded us here tonight with their strength and agility and their grace of motion? Folks, we are about to find out."

The crowd erupted again. The MC turned and looked at the girl on stage behind him.

He winked.

He lowered the microphone and said in an unamplified voice that sounded peculiar to her:

"Are you ready?"

He smiled kindly.

She nodded.

He gave her the A-OK sign with his fingers and nodded back. Then her lips broke open in return, disclosing, very slightly, her endearing gap-toothed smile.

He brought the microphone back to his mouth and turned again to the audience.

"Here we *go!*" he said.

The crowd went dead-silent in anticipation.

"Okay, okay!" she thought. All ten of her fingers wiggled unconsciously and in unison.

Abruptly, then, the lights above her darkened while simultaneously the lights behind her brightened, and then the music began: fast-paced and throbbing and happy.

She bolted forward.

She sprinted toward the balance beam and with astonishing speed executed a back handspring onto the springboard, vaulting into a full fluid backflip on one foot upon the beam — which in the very same motion turned into another back handspring, and then another, all to within inches of the bottles at the far end of the beam. This entire process took no more than five seconds. Here she paused for a fraction and then performed a half turn. From there she leapt lightly onto the first upright whiskey bottle, which wobbled only slightly under her weight. She placed her other toe catlike upon the next whiskey bottle, and then she raised herself en point to great heights....

2

SHE WAS CALLED DUSTY MAY. Her biological father, Winston Musgrave, whom she didn't know, was a Lakota acrobat of uncanny strength and coordination. For a time he was part of a traveling circus, which is when he met Dusty's mother Shonda — in Wendover, Nevada — while passing through. He had ropy arms and a vespine waist, and Dusty was conceived on a star-blown night in late May, along the outskirts of town, upon the canvas floor of a dusty tent where the circus was pitched. The next day he was gone.

Shonda, her pretty mother, also Lakota Sioux, carried Dusty to term, named her Dusty May and then, because of her poverty, gave her up for adoption.

This is how Dusty came to be raised in foster care.

Her foster father was a man named Kenneth Dvorak, a mighty Christian who, at six-foot-ten, three-hundred-thirty pounds, bald as a stone but handsome, commanded the attention of anyone whom he came in contact with. He was equal parts preacher, teacher, poet, politician, scientist — and over the years, he'd grown quite wealthy. He held an odd and eclectic political philosophy, which he wove intricately into his religion: a philosophy of sophisticated egalitarianism that was years in the making. He was also a widower. He had a large home in Templeton, Nevada, which home housed seven foster children and four of his own. He was a man of distinction. He spoke well. People argued about his modesty. His voice was rich and round and sonorously soothing. He had a special spot in his heart for Dusty May, who was the youngest of all his children, both biological and foster. He admired her silent determination, the unbreakable glint he saw in her infinitely black Lakota eyes. Shortly after Dusty turned thirteen, he began systematically raping her, though from the time she was a very young child, she'd been periodically molested by any number of her foster siblings.

Still, she remained a spirited girl who kindled and cultivated the glowing force at the core of her being, which she felt no one and no thing could ever damage or touch, because it lay burning so deeply inside her, and because it was all hers, because she had created it.

On a warm autumn day when Dusty was eight-years-old, looking out the window with a pair of binoculars her foster father had given her, she descried a young man walking tightrope-style around the thin cylindrical railing that circumscribed a nearby gymnasium. It was a large building and a long rail. He was walking the entire perimeter of the thing. He was stripped to the waist. He wore faded blue jeans. She'd never seen him before, and she stood at the window, the binoculars glued to her eyes, transfixed. He wasn't muscular but thin and graceful, not tall, brown-haired, swarthy, beautiful. She couldn't take her eyes off him. He didn't seem to be having any difficulty, yet it was such a long way around and such a thin rail that she expected at any moment he'd lose his balance and fall. But he never did. Banana-colored leaves see-sawed around him. She watched until he was finished.

When, at last, he came to the end, he did something that amazed her even more:

He leapt from the rail to a chainlink fence, some four feet to his right, and for a moment clung spider-like to the fence. Then he glided up to the top and from here, in one motion, vaulted over the fence, a full eight feet onto what she *thought* was the grassy ground.

Immediately, however, he came bouncing back up, high into the air, and then did a slow and effortless backflip, and kept bouncing. And bouncing. Dusty realized immediately what was happening:

A deep pit had been dug into the earth, a trampoline mat installed over the top of the pit.

Off to her left, in a large garden spread out below the window where she was, her foster father stood surveying his lands. For some reason, then — she did not know precisely why — she turned the binoculars around and looked at him through the wrong end. He was in life so large and looming, but suddenly he appeared very small. As suddenly, he turned to her, and, seeing her with her binoculars trained on him, he waved.

Watching him in this way, it looked to her as if a miniature person were waving at her from a vast distance.

Later that day, Dusty asked her foster father if she might be allowed to play on the trampoline, and he said yes.

So it began.

3

It BEGAN the morning after the evening Dusty asked her foster father for permission to play. He had always allowed her to roam, this mountainous man, though unknown to her, she was always watched, by him or by one of his men, among whom was a fellow named Wes Weekly, a devoted member of Kenneth Dvorak's congregation and also his friend. In fact, this very man owned the state-of-the-art gymnastics facility that comprised the trampolines, and he himself, no longer young, was in extraordinary physical condition. He personally coached the children.

Thus, this bright autumn morning, she made her way alone down the leafy lanes that led to his property — so excited that she several times broke into a sprint. Her maize-yellow tee-shirt read, in black block-print: RUN WILD.

There were three trampolines behind the fence, and she chose the one farthest away. A large white sign with red-stenciled letters said:

PLEASE REMOVE YOUR SHOES

Dusty slipped out of her sneakers and hopped sock-footed onto the trampoline mat. The daytime moon hung half-crumbled in the sky above, and the sky was burnished blue.

She began to jump. Her Indian-black hair lifted and fell. Soon she got her feet underneath her and grew more confident. She bounced higher and higher until, before long, she felt as though she were flying. After a while she half came to believe that the only thing preventing her from making it all the way up to the moon was her will and her will exclusively.

She was at it for some time before she realized she wasn't alone.

Observing her from grass, some twenty feet away, was the young man she'd watched spellbound through binoculars the day before.

He appeared suddenly, a friendly presence with a crooked smile and large brown eyes that were like blots of melting chocolate. He approached.

She stopped jumping.

He was at least nine years older than her. Immediately her eyes went to the long and wormy scar that ran the entire left side of his face clear down his neck, and he noticed her eyeing the scar.

"Admiring my seam?" he said. He cocked his head so that she might better see the length of it.

"It's a vacation souvenir I got four years ago, when I dove into a lake that I didn't know had rebar in it. I almost bled to death."

He leapt lightly onto the trampoline mat, and she stepped back.

"But I'm still standing!" he said.

He bounced once and landed on his knees and then

bounced back up onto his feet. He did it again. So relaxed, so natural-looking.

"Now you try it," he said.

She did it.

He smiled wider. He was one of the snaggle-toothed, the serene.

He told her his name was David. He said that he was the son of a woman named Bird, whose husband Wesson Weekly, his stepfather, owned the trampolines. He told her that he lived in Las Vegas with his father and stepmother, and that he was here only for a few days, as a visitor. She could feel his kindness: it radiated from him like a force-field. Indeed, it was largely this that gave her the courage to tell him she wanted to learn backflips and front flips, as she had seen him do the day before.

She held his gaze with some effort as she spoke.

He told her to watch closely, then. He said for her to pay attention to exactly what he was doing.

She stood off to the side, on the grass. He jumped. He spoke as he jumped, explaining everything while he did flips, both front and back. He spoke at length.

He told her that backflips are easier than front flips. He said that front flips are more dangerous. "Contrary to popular belief," he said.

He said that the most important thing to remember about *any* acrobatic maneuver is, first, you must fully decide and, second, you must fully follow through with that decision.

He said you must not overthink it, and you must not let your nerves get in the way.

He said that anything less than a total commitment to the move can cause injuries.

She listened to his every word, and she watched him

with lidless fixity. She thought that he was the most beautiful person she'd ever seen.

He said that, like most things, the first one you do is the most difficult. He said that after the first one, they all get easier.

He did backflip after backflip, slowly, effortlessly, describing to her precisely what he was doing and explaining to her the whole time precisely *how* he was doing it.

He told her once again that the most important thing for her to remember is to not hesitate after she decided to act. He said you decide and you act.

"And that," he said, ceasing, "is the whole secret of life."

He winked.

"Ready to try?"

She nodded.

"Would you like me to spot you?"

She shook her head.

"Okay."

He stepped off to one side, onto the grass, and with an open palm gestured for her to get on the trampoline.

He told her to do what she'd just watched him do.

She bounced several times, getting her feet back under her. He observed her. He did not say another word. He could see her thinking. He could feel her deciding. In an instant, then, as sudden as a bone-snap, she somersaulted backward and landed, a little overcorrected but safely, upon her feet. It took her two seconds before she realized that she had done it. It surprised her how easy it was.

He applauded.

She stood for a long moment, motionless and winded not so much from exertion as from the pure surge of adrenaline which came sloshing through her veins like nitroglycerin: the sense of limitless potential contained within her body and brain, the sudden knowledge of *that,* combined with the realization that she and she alone had done this thing, the touch of fear mixed with courage — it all converged in this moment and satisfied a secret hunger deep within her, something profound and poignant which she didn't know existed until right now, something inexpressibly private. She felt as though she'd been blasted out of a rocket-launcher.

"I think you've got the stuff," he said.

4

THE TOWN of Templeton lay in a river valley along the east-central edge of Nevada, about fifty miles west of the Utah border, a lorn but lovely sector of the state that even most Nevadans knew nothing of. The landscape itself, with its cirque-like bluffs and rarified air, exuded a pristine sparseness and sense of isolation, which Dusty May in her child's mind always likened to Andean crags and the strange Patagonian lands her foster mother had long ago read her stories about.

The Crystal River coursed down from the flinty hills ten miles to the east and flowed sinuously through the center of the village. The whole area was a hotbed of geothermal activity, webbed with a network of subsurface springs which bubbled up here and there all throughout the region. Long ago these springs had been harnessed and cultivated in many places around Templeton — which is why Wes Weekly's gymnasium contained eight circular tubs of graded temperature and a magnificent olympic-sized pool that was kept hyper-clean and cool for lap swimming.

Alone now and buoyant in the hottest of the hot tubs,

Dusty May couldn't stop thinking about the trampoline, the backflips, the brown-haired boy. Undreamed of vistas suddenly yawned open before her. She felt now that anything was possible, and this feeling gave her a euphoric rush the likes of which she'd never experienced. She could not repress her smile, her gap-tooth grin. Her thin brown legs undulated below her in the rippled water. Her big eyes glowed with life. She stared at her legs and thought of the bones and blood and muscles they contained. Her inky hair hung damp and beaded. The water was so hot that she felt as though she were being boiled alive slowly. She stood it for as long as she could and then emerged steaming and dove headlong into the icy swimming pool, her powerful little heart hammering.

5

THE NEXT FOUR YEARS, every day virtually without exception, she practiced the slippery art of gymnastic balance: she burned through boxes of athletic tape, tube after tube of gooey salve, conical blocks of hand-chalk.

In the early morning, she swam laps in Wes Weekly's olympic-sized pool.

In the evening, she tumbled and swung and negotiated the balance beam.

The swimming was her idea.

She practiced indefatigably. She practiced and she learned. Among other things, she learned greater discipline and discovered, in a manner that struck her rather like the dawning of a revelation, that the better she got, the greater her desire grew: her desire for skill. In this way, her passion for the thing was incremental and willed. The moment she explicitly grasped this, her entire view of human existence was recast and restructured in her mind.

Thus, over the course of six years, she grew increasingly certain that in every significant area, her destiny was under her own control.

This newly developed knowledge armed her in a subtle but insurmountable way.

PART II

6

One dark December day, when Dusty May was eleven-years-old, a muscular and mean-looking Latin youth, perhaps twenty-seven, cross-hatched with facial scars and covered in prison tats, who was part of a roving carnival and who was manning one of the games Dusty was playing, asked her in rapid Spanish, and with a wink and a lewd look, where that gap between her two front teeth came from — and then in the same breath, he asked her if she was Mexican or Indian or half-breed, or did she even know.

The man did not expect her to understand, but her foster father Kenneth Dvorak had taught her to speak Spanish, and she spoke it well, and now she answered the man in kind — or, rather, she started to:

Before she had time to finish her answer, her foster father appeared as if from nowhere — and in a phenomenal blur of speed and force, without any hesitation or compunction whatsoever, he hammered the young man with an iron-like right fist directly on the young man's ear, and then again with a left: hammered him violently, smashing the young man's jaw to smithereens, so that before he collapsed onto the straw-carpeted ground, the young man drooled out a huge mouthful of blood and teeth.

In the same motion, Kenneth Dvorak swept Dusty up into his arms and carried her safely away. The whole incident lasted no more than sixty seconds.

Later that same evening, he explained to her in his rich round voice that her racial pedigree, as everyone's racial pedigree, is meaningless — because race, he said, is unchosen.

He told her to always remember this. "Always," he repeated.

He told her that anyone placing any essential importance upon her race or skin color, whether in denigration or commendation, is espousing a form of racism, which, he said, is a type of collectivism — but a type, he told her, of the most barbarous kind — and as such it seeks to ascribe moral significance to an unchosen aspect of the human condition: genetic chemistry and the automatic amalgamation of our DNA codes, which in actuality fall completely outside the realm of choice.

He told her that humans are defined and therefore united by one thing alone, and that is the human faculty of reason, which is the rational faculty, and that this faculty is activated and maintained by an act of choice — choice being the very locus of moral action, he said, and without which no deed can be deemed either moral or immoral because if there is no choice, all deeds by definition are amoral.

He said that all humans who are born healthy, regardless of race or skin color or sex or sexual orientation, possess this faculty, and he said that to define humans by anything other than the rational faculty, whether by race, sex, color, class, or gender, is an attempt to bestow moral worth in the absence of any moral action one way or the other, and that it is also an attempt to define by means of non-essential characteristics, which, he said, is to define incorrectly.

He told her that such an attempt will only ever serve to divide people endlessly — divide and subdivide, he said — and then he quoted something to her, in a lilting language she didn't understand:

Lo maggior don che Dio per sua larghezza
   fesse creando, e a la sua bontate
   più conformato, e quel ch'e' più apprezza,
   fu de la volontà la libertate;
   di che le creature intelligenti,
   e tutte e sole, fuore e son dotate.

"The greatest gift which God in His bounty bestowed in creating, and the most conformed to His own goodness and that which He most prizes, was the freedom of the will, with which the creatures that have intelligence, they all and they alone, were and are endowed," he said.

Kenneth Dvorak told Dusty that life is action and action is movement, and that humans are defined by their actions, not their blood or race or racial ancestry or sex or gender, and that actions are shaped by thoughts, and thinking is activated or not by an act of choice.

"And what is mind," he quoted, "but movement in the intellectual sphere?"

Thereafter, Dusty May thought not at all about her Lakota blood.

AND YET THROUGHOUT that small area, the "little Lakota orphan" became known for her strength and her skill — the girl with silken black hair who won gymnastics contests and the affections of everybody. Or almost everybody.

One man alone in the township of Templeton kept himself free from any affection for Dusty May, and no matter her discipline, no matter her sweetness of disposition, he remained indifferent to her and aloof.

That man was Wesson Weekly, her teacher.

Weekly belonged to that race of monstrous yet remarkable men who, if ordered to do so by a superior — someone to whom he'd pledged his total allegiance, which he did only rarely and with great caution — he'd hold his arm over a blowtorch until the flame burned a hole clean through.

He had the psychology of a cyborg, pure and unassailable, which creates peculiar sympathies and antipathies, and which is all of a piece, never perturbed, never in doubt, never able to conceive of being wrong.

Around his home and his businesses, he was above nothing and never asked anyone to perform any task he wouldn't do himself. He therefore did everything: cleaned toilets and bathroom stalls, mopped floors, laundry, cooking, dishes. But he was always unquestionably the one in command.

His wife — ten children later and past her prime — still retained a vestige of her former loveliness. She was silent and passive and existed purely to please him.

Weekly never drank.

He never smoked.

He never used drugs.

He was born in a brothel. His mother was a Nevada prostitute who had no husband and who, drug-addled and sick, died shortly after he'd slid screaming from the bone-carved womb.

He was thus raised in an orphanage and grew up thinking of himself cut-off and shut-off from normalized society. As a child and all throughout his childhood he secretly despaired of ever entering it.

He was just over medium height and extraordinarily strong. He kept a military-like regimen of exercise, as he had all his life, for the orphanage that raised him instituted just such a regimen. At age eighteen, he entered the army.

He spent the next ten years of his life there: a special-forces soldier who saw a great deal of combat and blood.

His face was wedge-shaped and gaunt. He was unusual-looking yet handsome. He had an upturned nose the nostrils of which appeared bored-out with an auger. He kept his sandy-colored hair cropped close to the skull — not a crew-cut but high-and-tight — just as he had all through his military career, the sideburns perfectly symmetrical and neatly trimmed, shaped like a miniature pair of pointy cowboy boots. He was otherwise clean-shaven.

One felt ill-at-ease gazing too long into the dark caves of

his nostrils, which in a strange sort of way aped his all-pupil eyes that were so dark and baleful-looking, enshadowed by the eaves of his brow-ridge.

When he smiled, which was infrequently, his lips pulled back and up simultaneously in such a way as to expose his gums and his big square teeth. It gave him a kind of crazed-horse look.

He had one overwhelming weakness, and that was his crippling fear of heights, which his entire adult life he'd striven to overcome, but never successfully. He often dreamt of suddenly finding himself astronomically high among the cauliflower clouds, up in the stratosphere, atop a balance beam, the earth below a tiny blue ball like a planet viewed through the wrong end of a telescope, and he so paralyzed with fear that he must crawl his way along the beam, inching, utterly terrified.

Distilled down to his essence, he was the seamless integration of two sentiments, both of which in and of themselves were unremarkable and even common, but in him they were taken to such extremes that they'd become abominable — arrant loyalty to authority and arrant antipathy for its opposite: unbridled freedom.

In some way he couldn't quite identify but which he unquestionably felt and over which he even lost sleep, Dusty May, his best student ever, represented this latter thing.

ON A MONUMENTAL MORNING shortly after she turned
sixteen, Dusty May came across an old photo in her father's
library. She discovered it inside a torn magazine, among a
box of discards. The photo depicted, in beautiful black-and-
white, a young ballerina walking en point atop a row of
wine bottles. The ballerina wore a cat mask and black
leotards. She was very lovely. When Dusty's eyes fell upon
the photo, she felt herself whisked away to a strange and
magical universe: a universe of endless fascination.

She examined the photo microscopically.

She sought to know more about this remarkable human
who walked like a cat upon the upright bottles. But there
was no actual article and no real information, apart from a
name and a date in the bottom left corner:

"German Ballerina Bianca Passarge, 1958."

It intrigued her in a way she couldn't describe, even to
herself.

She went to his library several times a day for a week
straight just to look at the photo, until, before she quite

knew it, a radical idea had hatched open inside her head: an idea which in equal measure exhilarated and terrified her.

After that, she spent a great deal of time reading books about ballet. She read in the quick gliding manner her foster father had taught her, for Dusty was born severely dyslexic, and ten years had passed before she was diagnosed — by Kenneth Dvorak: the act of reading up to that point sheer torture for her, until Dvorak, alone among her teachers and elders, discovered the root of her difficulties, and then showed her an ingenious way to overcome it: a method of reading he himself had devised.

More than anything, though, Dusty loved looking at the photographs of all the beautiful dancers.

She was astonished to discover their feats of sheer strength, which she indeed knew something of, but in her eyes their strength was mixed with refinement and pure poise, which she felt she lacked.

Over a period of ten days, without quite realizing it, this was something she came to see as an explicit metaphor for her own life: strength and poise in perfect harmony and balance with each other.

She wanted that for herself.

She wanted it now more than she'd ever wanted anything.

And so it was on the 2nd of August, 2005, about one hour before sunset, this waifish-looking girl with defiant eyes and a gap-toothed smile stood at the third-story window of the huge mansion in which she'd been brought up — the presence of the man who owned it, her foster father Kenneth Dvorak, thundering silently throughout its hallways, and the hallways of her head.

She was not smiling now.

She stared across the lumpy landscape spread out below

her. A reef of clouds stood piled on the western horizon. Purple thunderheads hung static curtains of rain. Her brows were knitted in stormy thought.

It was here, watching the sun go down, that she made her final decision.

She ran away.

Shortly after which, the little creatures visited her.

WHEN KENNETH DVORAK AWOKE, he knew before he was consciously aware of it that something was amiss.

He lay alone in his bed. The room was suffused in a murky sea-colored light. He slept in the nude, as was his habit. His vast corpus tilted the mattress when he turned onto his back. He lay for a time squinting in thought at the huge beams of maplewood smothered in shadow across his high ceiling. On his desk beyond, there were petri dishes and a large, technological-looking microscope. He folded his covers back into a large dog-ear and swung his legs out of bed.

He put on his robe and went to Dusty's room.

She was not there.

Her bed was made and empty.

He went straight to the telephone and called up Wesson Weekly, whose wife Bird answered.

"Hello?"

"This is Kenneth."

"I was just getting ready to call you."

"Why?"

"Wes isn't here."

"Where is he?"

"I don't know. He was gone when I woke."

"Is David back?"

"David?"

"Yes, dammit, David."

"No," she said, "he's not. He hasn't been back in over a year."

10

THE BELLS of Saint John struck six the moment she emerged from the depot. She hurried down the city sidewalks, a small swift figure in a mushroom-shaped cap that partially hid her face, large catlike sunglasses, which hid her face even more, black jeans and a denim jacket with a high cut, a small black backpack on her back. Her hair was tucked under her cap, and this gave her an almost boyish mien. She paused only once to glance behind her — as though she suddenly sensed she was being followed. She saw nothing, however, except empty streets and vaporous sidewalks — and yet deep inside her mind, she could not shake the feeling that she was being pursued. Ragged ghosts of carbolic mist blew over her.

Before facing forward, she lifted her eyes briefly to the sky. She surveyed the heavens. The tolling bell struck again. It struck her heart with a gothic pang. Bats were doing square root over the tarnished towers to the west. She scanned the sky for a moment, as though something were perhaps watching her from above. But the pewter sky was empty, save for the swarming bats and, much higher overhead, a solitary hawk describing slow parabolas across the void.

She continued on.

She walked purposefully in her black sneakers, her shoulders straight, a sure and confident walk, especially in one so young — a walk that disclosed the great familiarity she had with her own physicality. Yet her hands were sweating and clammy, her fingers trembling, which she noticed only now. She balled them into little fists and stuffed them like two kidneys into the thin pockets of her jacket.

The pewter light poured down around her in rippled sheets.

She increased her speed. She was walking vaguely east. She passed by a building with boarded-up windows, and in front of this building a beggar crouched upon the sidewalk. He was wrapped in black rags and bent in mute supplication or prayer. In her backpack she carried a detailed map of the city — a map she'd striven to memorize — and still she felt slightly confused and turned-around and unsure of her way.

By and by, she came to a fountain thundering water in the middle of a vast city square. The square was deserted. The plash of the falling water soothed her. A cool breeze came off the water and carried with it small dapples of moisture that flecked her face. She stopped walking and looked behind her again. She rotated a slow 360 degrees, her dark eyes narrowed behind her dark glasses. The square was so big that she could scarcely make out the other side. She saw no one. She unshouldered her pack and retrieved the map and familiarized herself anew.

The carillon continued its dolorous toll.

11

——

Not thirty minutes later, a quarter-mile back in the direction she'd just walked, she came to a dance-studio — and here, in a moment of total devastation, the plan she'd just staked her entire life upon came apart in a monumentally silent explosion.

This studio was owned by a famous ballet teacher, about whom she'd read much: a man she'd never met nor even set eyes upon, but a man she planned on walking right up to, showing him the photo of the magical human who danced catlike upon the wine bottles, and saying to him, "Will you teach me how to do this?"

When, however, she came to the numbered address of the famous dance-studio, she saw immediately why she'd passed by it a half-hour before without seeing it: the name and sign were stripped, the windows boarded up, the dance-studio closed.

She peered in through the tinted glass of the front door.

Through the darkness, far back, she saw strips of yellow police tape and chalk lines on the floor outlining the shape of a human body.

12

IT WAS GETTING DARKER, but there was still plenty of daylight. The light was curiously sharp. She re-coordinated. She backtracked. She started toward the fountain again, but then she changed her mind. She walked back down the block that the abandoned studio was on. Here she again passed by the beggar in black. For some reason, then, she did not know why, it came to her suddenly, and with a great shock, that a few days before she'd run away from her home, she'd written the name of this dance studio on a soft paper-pad, the imprint of which had perhaps bled through.

Had it bled through?

And if it had, what now could she do?

Her eyes went back to the beggar. He was still crouched in silent supplication, but the instant she looked at him, he lifted his head, and for a brief but intense moment he gazed directly into her eyes. His movement was like the flash of a blade. She shuddered and caught her breath.

In that moment, in the wan and knifey twilight, though his hat was pulled down over his forehead and his face was streaked with dirt, it seemed to her that she recognized him.

She experienced the sensation of one unexpectedly face-to-face with a deadly beast.

For a split second, she felt herself unable to move or breathe at all and, horror-stricken, she saw a blinding explosion of white, like a bolt of lightning blazing across the blackness of her brain. She went dizzy and even felt herself totter. Through her dark glasses, she stood staring at the man, who had lowered his head again. She did not breathe or speak. She thought:

This cannot be, this is not real, I must be dreaming.

At last, she felt herself able to move, and she hurried on.

13

SHE CAME at length to the local youth hostel some two miles away. With a wad of cash that she'd saved over the course of years, she paid for a private room, and that first night passed without incident — until she slept.

Late that night, she fell into an uncommonly deep slumber, and while she slept, an army of little creatures, almost microscopic, marched into her room, under her door, and they climbed up her bed and streamed inside her body, entering her through all her cavities. They infiltrated her.

She was fully aware of these tiny creatures, as she was aware also that they had been created by her scientific foster father Kenneth Dvorak, who, Godlike, had sought all his adult life to bring inanimate things into being, who had animated these beings into moving things from inorganic matter, who had somehow discovered a way to breathe vital breath — his own breath, perhaps — into non-living entities, who had devised something mysterious and phenomenal in his lab of making.

"What lives?" he now said to her. His thunderous voice, sourceless and unbidden, resounded around the bone concavity of her skull. "And what is life if not motion, and what is mind if not motion in the sphere of the intellect?"

The little beings poured thickly inside her even as he spoke inside her mind. They poured into her external flesh and dispersed throughout her internal body, and when at last they were all inside her, they began to go to work on her bones and tissues and all her living organs, but at a cellular level, deep, deep down inside her body, seeking to demolish her little by little, breaching the integrity of her bones and her whole person: her body enmeshed with her brain. They sought one-by-one to dismantle the living components of her flesh-and-bone, which made her animate and alive, and it was only with a great effort of her mind and her will that she could defend herself from within. The glowing force at her core which was her essence remained an impregnable field, though it was at this that they hammered away most violently — hammered and blasted and rammed and chipped.

She lay upon her bed only partially asleep, absolutely aware the whole time what was happening, yet nonetheless totally paralyzed, unable to move a single muscle in her entire living body — except once, with extraordinary effort, she was able to just slit open her eyes for a moment, and then her leaden lids slammed shut again.

By means of her brain and her brain alone was she able to fight this army of tiny creatures which her foster father had unleashed in his laboratory of germ warfare and arcane devisings, and fight this army she did.

She did.

14

THE NEXT EVENING, around nine, while she sat alone in her room thinking and recalculating, she heard the door of the hostel open two floors below. It opened, she thought, with an ominous creak and then came footsteps, directly after which she heard a masculine voice that sounded to her deliberately hushed.

After that, for a brief time, all was silent as before. Then the sound of footsteps resumed. They were coming up the stairs toward her room. She sat completely still. The lights in her room were off, the room darkling. She glanced at the door. It was bolted and chained, upon noticing which, she felt a rush of relief pour through her.

She listened closely.

The floors of the hostel were old and wooden. They creaked with rocking-chair moans under the slow-creeping steps, which sounded heavy: the footsteps of a man.

She stared at the door.

She did not make the slightest movement or sound. She fixed her eyes on the keyhole through which she could see a star of beaming light.

Suddenly, that star of light was extinguished, as though something had blotted it out— and in that moment she knew without any doubt that a person was looking in through her keyhole. But all the lights were off, and her room was smothered in velvety darkness. She did not breathe.

After half a minute, that gleaming star of light reappeared, and she again heard the masculine footsteps creak and then recede.

But a moment after that, she heard also this same person checking into the room directly next to hers.

FULLY CLOTHED AND SILENT, a silently moving girl, she lay back on her pillow and tried to calm her brain. She attempted to rest, but she was unable to even shut her eyes.

She lay like this for a long time, her mind swarming in wild surmise.

Outside, the crickets in the trees stridulated with such demonic ferocity that they sounded to her as if they might saw themselves in half. A breeze the size of a child's ankle blew over her. It parted the cloth curtains. Beyond, in the low-hanging sky, dove-gray clouds were pulling slowly apart, a solitary star winking there with a cold and greenish light.

She stared at it.

She stared at it for a long time, and she thought of a quote Kenneth Dvorak had once written in a notebook he'd given her:

"I have always loved the stars too fondly to be fearful of the night."

She thought of her foster father and how he alone had taught her to read, his own method by means of which she was at last able to match written symbols with sound, and she thought also of certain missives he'd written her, when he was away: kind, thoughtful, often profound letters in his beautiful quick handwriting, which she'd come to love. She thought of one of those letters now, from years ago:

You are a star — this letter said — *a rare and precious star. Don't you know? Do not ever let it go, and do not ever forget. Do not get mired in mediocrity, or let yourself live in bondage to banality. Dusty May, you were meant for more. You were meant to soar.*

Even after everything, recalling his words anew she *felt* the sincerity in his voice — because he was sincere, because he loved her so. As she loved him.

As he had spoken many such things to her.

Alone in the youth hostel and thinking of it now, the inexpressibly complicated feeling of pure ambivalence that she knew so well tore through her again unbidden, perhaps for the millionth time in her life: the sense of sheer love mixed with sheer revulsion she had for him, who was so good to her so often, who had done so much that was good and gentle and kind, who had even once, when Dusty was twelve and fell wading across a river and was sucked down in the rapid current and had actually drowned, resuscitated her, breathing life back in her — who loved her so deeply in return and yet who had committed such unspeakable acts of violation.

She lay in thought. Her eyes were wide open: deep black pools liquid with life and a furious defiance.

She was startled out of reverie by the sound of footsteps

coming up the steps and approaching. These steps, less heavy-sounding, were creeping toward her door.

Was it the young woman who had checked her into this room, who had been kind to her?

She sat up.

At the base of her door glowed a luminous strip of light.

Through this strip of light a folded piece of paper suddenly appeared.

Then the footsteps receded, and now an even heavier silence descended over everything — a silence which her slightest movement would crumble into dust.

She stared long at the paper on the floor, before she at last rose to retrieve it. Still, she did not pick it up. She stood in the middle of the room. She seemed hesitant to reach down and lift the note up off the floor, as if a part of her would rather not know its cryptic contents.

16

HOGAN PHILLIPS, the forensic psychologist, six-foot-five-inches tall and weighing two-hundred-sixty pounds, leaned back in his oak swivel chair and stared out his study-room window. The chair crepitated beneath his bulk with an almost human-like sound. His view ran across a long lush garden of creamy daisies and magenta Morning Glories and then into a series of variegated fields. A profound stillness hung in the air, an enchanted quality creeping in with the mist, the seamless sky hourless, slate-blue: an unbroken bell adumbrating rain.

His coffee cup stood steaming on his desk. He reached for it now and took a careful sip. The room was warm.

He was half-Cherokee, half-black, and at fifty-five-years-old, he'd never felt sharper, stronger, surer. He still had a full head of hair, moon-colored, which he wore cropped short, the forelock dangling over his left eye like a wave about to capsize.

Never married, though a great lover of the female flesh, Hogan Phillips maintained now an almost ascetical lifestyle, as he had for the last fifteen years of his life. Over the long arc of his life as well, he'd developed the tear-ducts of the chronic insomniac, the bloodshot eyes of the habitual ruminator.

He'd initially tried to battle his insomnia by reading more — big books deep into the night: dense tomes of forensic, philosophic, or economic literature.

When that didn't work, he intensified his level of exercise: a religious regimen, which he kept to this day, of dips and push-ups, pull-ups off his warm basement bars, a huge man bowing the creaking pipes of plumbing beneath his home, and then long runs into the iron dawn.

He stared now through his large plate-glass window. The August evening was collapsing into night. The air hung green and gauzy. Presently he heard, from around the other side of the house, out of his view, a car crackle up his white-gravel driveway, and he checked his watch.

He took another sip of coffee.

Then he rose up from his moaning chair and went to the front door to meet his noctivagant visitor.

THE YOUNG MAN on his doorstep had brown hair and chocolate-brown eyes so large and wet-looking that they
reminded Hogan of a stuffed elk. He had a long scar down
one side of his face. He stood drenched in the sodium porch
light. He was medium height, flat-stomached and uncommonly lean but muscular, with arms like a gymnast — or a
wrestler, thought former high-school heavyweight state-
champion Hogan Phillips.

From his doorstep, Hogan eyed his visitor with great
interest. The winding white-gravel driveway glowed ghostly
beyond.

In sheer size, Hogan dwarfed him, but there was a
certain aura about the young man, apart from his obvious
fitness — an excess of energy, an overwhelming sense of
healthiness, which set the young man apart and gave him
an indescribably formidable presence.

They shook hands in silence, and then Hogan led the
young man down a short hallway that opened up into his
living room. In the other direction, a steep staircase
descended into eerie blackness. The living room was

spacious and bare to the point of minimalism. It was lit with a soft eggshell light. A whisper of lavender laced the air. Outside, the mist was oozing in across the fields.

The young man stood for a moment upon the threshold. His shoes were lead-gray and had flat soles. He scanned the room slowly. Hogan gestured with an open palm for the young man to sit. But the young man did not immediately do so. Hogan watched him: the strange isolated healthiness of the young man's body. Hogan offered him a drink, which the young man declined. Overhead, the electric light flickered once, and in distance came the long sad wail of the train.

At slight length, the young man moved to the chair Hogan had offered. He seated himself and crossed his legs smoothly, left over right. Hogan sat opposite him, an ash coffee table between them.

"Thank you for making time," the young man said.

"It is my pleasure."

"You have a beautiful home."

"Thank you."

"I didn't realize it was quite like this out here."

"Quite like what?"

"Calm and peaceful."

"Yes. That gets into your blood."

"The quiet?"

"The stillness, yes," Hogan said, "the serenity."

They were both silent for a moment.

"Are you retired from your official work, Mr. Phillips?"

"Hogan, please. No, I still work."

"What exactly does a forensic psychologist do?"

"Different things. In a general sense, a forensic psychologist provides psychological insight into legal matters, both criminal and civil."

"You are criminal, though, correct — a criminal-forensic psych?"

"Yes, I am. Initially I studied agriculture. Then anthropology. First and foremost, I regard myself as a forensic anthropologist."

"Oh?"

"Yes."

"But you switched to psychology?"

"I do both. Body and brain."

"What do you mean?"

"I mean that forensic anthropology is the physical-anatomical aspect of the same profession. Psychology studies a person's psychological-subconscious motivations."

"Have you always run a private practice?"

"Yes. I'm primarily hired by law enforcement to help the investigative process. But I'm hired by other people as well."

"You do missing-person work too?"

"Yes. Not often, but yes."

The young man nodded and his wet-looking cow eyes went philosophically to the floor.

Outside, the darkness was nearly accomplished. Reflected ghost-like upon Hogan's windowpanes, their seated figures appeared to be hovering just above the foggy fields.

"Do you know what the first rule of forensic psychology is?" Hogan said.

"No."

"As people do one thing, so they do everything."

"That's Buddhist," the young man said.

"Yes, I believe it is."

"Why is it the number one rule of forensic psychology?"

"Because people's behavior in one area invariably manifests in other areas. It doesn't operate in so isolated or compartmentalized a fashion as most people reckon. Because we do what we repeatedly desire, what we repeatedly think, and we are what we repeatedly do."

"Faithful in a little, faithful in a lot."

"Yes."

"Do you see this sort of thing often?"

"What?"

"People's behavior in one area coming out in other areas."

"I see it all the time."

The young man was silent.

"It's been said that the second half of a person's life consists largely of living with the habits developed during the first," Hogan said. "Most people are a mix: we operate along a spectrum, and that spectrum is fluid. The question is a question of degrees. But the values and habits we develop when we're young unquestionably shape us for the rest of our lives. And good principles drive out bad. This is true in every sphere of life: political, economic, psychological, epistemological, ethical."

The young man considered this. Hogan eyed the complicated plexus of veins like webs on each of the young man's forearms.

"Be careful what you learn to love," the young man said. "Life is barely long enough to master one thing."

"What is that?"

"Something I once read."

"It is well said."

"Do you believe authentic change in a person is possible later in life?"

"Yes. But difficult."

"What does it require? Fundamentally?"

"A sincere and unremitting desire, fundamentally."

"You've seen many bad things," the young man said. It was not quite a question.

"Yes. So many. So bad."

"What does that word mean to a forensic psychologist?"

"Bad?"

"Yes."

"Things harmful to human flourishing and human life, which is not just physical but psychological. The bad is that which stunts and frustrates this, in both the doer and the receiver."

"A psychological definition of evil I once heard — psychological as opposed to religious — is vanity and laziness taken to a deeper level."

"Perhaps. One thing concerning this subject I've definitely come to understand over the years: the more extreme a person's desires and values, the more those desires and values shape the person's essence."

"What do you mean?"

"One cannot easily think of truly pathological people as fundamentally anything but. The extreme nature of their values precludes it because these radical values define them completely. It becomes their essence, no matter what else they like and love and do."

The young man took a moment to consider this, as well. Then, very abruptly, he produced a crinkled note from the breast pocket of his tee-shirt. He passed it to Hogan Phillips, who opened it and saw, in strange thrusting letters, these words:

"He has done unspeakable things. I am running."

For some time, Hogan studied the note, as well as the paper, and then he looked up at the young man. "What is this?" he said.

"Something that was recently sent to me."

"Has it come to pass?"

"Yes."

"You said on the phone that you wanted to meet with me because you had questions about the foster father of the girl," Hogan said.

"Yes. That is why I'm here."

"I'll answer them if I can."

The young man nodded. "Thank you," he said.

18

"How long did you know Kenneth Dvorak?" the young man asked.

"A long time," Hogan said. "Since we were children." Hogan paused thoughtfully.

The young man watched him.

"He is ..." Hogan said. He paused again.

"Yes?"

"A peculiar fellow. I'm not exaggerating when I tell you that I've never known anybody remotely like him."

"How so?"

Hogan took another long moment. The house creaked around them.

"It's difficult to put into precise words," he said at last. "We're the same age, and I've known him since I was seven-years-old, and yet I'm sincere when I say I don't really have any better understanding of him now than I did then."

"Were you friends?"

"Yes."

There was another long pause. The scorching wail of a

locomotive cut through the dead silence beyond. Creamy mist lay folded over the clover fields.

"At one time, in fact, we were close friends," Hogan said, "insofar as anyone can really be close friends with Kenneth."

"You grew up together?"

"Yes. We were in elementary, junior high, and high school together — and then we were in the same agriculture school. Our personalities and our worldview were always quite different, but we did share something fundamental in common — though I'm still not sure precisely what that thing was."

"What do you mean?"

"We had a certain connection that none of the others had, but it was so subtle that it's very difficult to pinpoint. I've thought a lot about this. I've never really gotten to the bottom of it. Still, it did give us a delicate but unmistakable bond. Also, we both began our careers at the same time, and we were in the Army at the same time. Professionally, we both advanced at approximately the same pace as well, and excelled. He grew up on a farm, as did I. In fact, his father was a somewhat famous and innovative farmer, and Kenneth himself was an incredibly hard-worker, even when he was very young. He had a way of doing things that was always slightly unorthodox but oddly smart — smart in a way that made you think: how obvious. And yet it also made you think that you wouldn't have thought of it in a hundred years."

"Can you give me an example?"

"He invented his own form of math to solve certain engineering problems on the farm. And this was when he was just a teenager. Look here: I was a math person too — I've

always liked numbers and math — and yet I never understood his methods. And not for want of trying, either. Yet
you can see the internal logic in them."

The young man didn't say anything but went deeper into
contemplation.

"Kenneth was far more driven than me or anyone I
knew, and perhaps inordinately brilliant because of how
driven he was. And make no mistake: he *is* brilliant. He's
also a very private person, even among his family, and I
don't even think his wife knew him fully."

"No?"

Hogan shook is head.

"How did she die?"

"His wife?"

"Yes."

"A car accident. She drowned."

"There were rumors – "

"Unsubstantiated."

Another brief silence fell.

Over the raggedy horizon to the east, a huge hump-
backed moon crept up and stood brooding and rust-colored
over the western world.

"You were saying you thought not even his wife knew
him in full."

"Yes. That is what I think. Though we grew up together,
Kenneth's childhood is shadowy. I knew him in elementary
school, but not outside of it. He was raised in a deeply religious home, back when that religion still had a lot of 'the
old salt in it,' as he once put it to me. I think I remember this
description verbatim after forty-five years because I liked it.
And yet somewhere along the line, after seminary or even
while he was still in school, his religious convictions began
rather rapidly to shift."

"Shift in what way?"

"Kenneth was always an incredible reader — I mean, encyclopedic — more than anyone I've ever known, and this is not an exaggeration. No matter how much you guess he's read, I promise you'll underestimate it."

"Oh?"

"Yes. And last I knew he spoke twenty-two different languages, and spoke them well — all self-taught. He can write Arabic, Chinese, Japanese, and Cyrillic. More than anything, he's indefatigably thoughtful. He won't rest until he's followed an idea to its conclusion. This is one of the things I liked most about him."

"Because you saw yourself in it," said the young man, who not only knew Hogan Phillips, but knew quite a lot about him, from reading his work — knew and admired him.

Hogan appeared to take no notice of these last words, however.

"Around age thirty-three — and this is my point," Hogan said, "when he was engaged in so much reading and study, his religious convictions started tilting toward the political."

"Do you mean that his religious convictions gave way to the political and then took the place of?"

"No, I don't mean that. But that is the right question to ask."

"What do you mean, then?"

"I mean that he began to fuse his religious convictions with his political, and in this way you could say he created a new sort of religious order. Also at this time, his interest in agriculture and genetic modification went to another level. I know this because it was then that he ceased seeing people at all, myself included. In fact, the last time I ever saw Kenneth was in his lab."

"What was he doing?"

"He'd figured out a way to introduce genes into a certain type of bean plant. After the genes were introduced, they coaxed the plants into producing micronutrients of beta carotene and homocysteine, which the human body then converts into vitamin A and vitamin B. Kenneth also managed in this same bean plant to create a genetically modified version that was resistant to disease. It was ingenious and even his detractors concede that in this area of bio-genetic chemistry and agriculture, among others, he's exceptional."

Hogan fell momentarily mute. The young man continued to watch him.

"One of the last things Kenneth told me in person," Hogan said, "is that he'd found a way to (as he put it) 'animate inanimate matter.'"

"What did he mean by that?"

"That he'd solved the problem of how single-cellular life could arise naturally on planet earth from a complicated soup of non-living chemicals and other inanimate matter."

"Is it true?"

"I don't know. But it would not surprise me. Some people believed also that he was engaged at this time in highly illegal activity: specifically, the creation and cultivation of viruses and deadly germs, even preparing an arsenal for germ warfare. It was a real rumor, and I myself have never entirely discounted it."

The young man didn't speak.

"To your initial question," Hogan said, "I knew Kenneth as well as anyone. And I know that he overcame a great deal of hostility and adversity and harassment." Here, for the first time in this conversation, Hogan's voice and face grew dramatic. *"Extraordinary* amounts," he added. "And this included his foiling a number of plots to destroy his lab by bomb or arson. Kenneth was not cowed, however. Of all people, he would never be cowed or bullied. One simply can't imagine it. As a matter of fact, it almost seemed as though he was ready for it. There was even a shootout Kenneth was involved in, protecting his research and his property, a shootout in which people died — Kenneth killed them — and for which Kenneth was exonerated on the grounds of a self-defense and protection of his property."

"I recall reading about that," the young man said.

"Yes. All his acquaintances without exception — myself foremost among them — were therefore shocked when he bought a huge area of land near a depopulated village in eastern Nevada, land he was able to purchase because this village was on the brink of ghost-town, and here he started his strange little church, which was founded in agriculture and his own religion, and which grew rapdily."

"Strange in what way?"

"What I alluded to before."

"Which was?"

"The religious doctrine being very vague on the notion of God, but explicitly political, and the methods of farming so much in line with those who were diametrically opposed to his genetically modified plants. Kenneth understood agriculture as thoroughly as any living person, and he understood as well the importance of organic matter — in the true sense of that word."

"Make that clearer."

"He understood, as all Ag students do, the importance of organic matter as a component of the soil — and under-

stood also that soil fertility and the kind of crops you grow
on a soil are not determined by humus alone."

"In this I'm not knowledgeable," said the young man.

"Soil fertility is determined by the amount of active
organic matter, the amount of available mineral nutrients,
the activities of soil organisms, chemical activities in the soil
solution and the physical condition of the soil — none of
which is new data: humans have understood it for a very
long time. Ever since we've had soil scientists, they have
recognized the values of organic matter. But I know for a
fact that Kenneth always felt as though a perfectly good
word — 'organic' — had been taken and appropriated and
stretched to cover an entire doctrine most of which fell
completely outside the bounds of that word. He also
believed that there was really no such thing as 'unnatural'
and that synthetic and natural were purely a question of
form."

"I see," the young man said. "And so when he bought up
such vast amounts of land and started this farm, you were
surprised."

"That's hardly the word for it. But almost immediately,
he began making money — the farm itself began making
money — and a great deal of it. Before he'd even begun,
he'd set up an inexpensive infrastructure for distribution
and for advertising the farms diverse food products."

"The farm flourished."

"Yes. As did his flock. And the doctrine Kenneth
founded was steeped as much in economics and agriculture
as it was in morality and God. Kenneth then discovered oil
on his land, and he began cultivating that too. So that the
farm soon moved completely off the grid. I believe part of
him actually wanted to secede from the nation, and this also
is why I've never entirely discounted the rumors of germ

warfare. And yet his farm wasn't communistic — at least, not totally. The last time I tried to visit him, before he shut me out for good, I got the definite sense that Kenneth sought to control people not through property but by means of some other thing or way."

"What other thing or way?"

"I don't know. Some deeper method: as he modified genes, I often thought, from deep within at the fundamental level, beyond the cellular, so he sought to modify the total individual, which he once told me with a smile was 'merely a tiny part of a much larger organic whole.' Unquote."

Hogan paused.

"But to tell the God's honest truth," he continued, "I never thought he believed this doctrine. At all."

"Which?" the young man said.

"The religion he preaches, and its economic-political counterpart."

"No? Then what was he in it for? Money?"

"No." Hogan again fell silent, appeared to ponder. "I don't know what he was in it for, but I do know that it wasn't money or fame."

"Depth of conviction, perhaps, combined with the fervor he had for his religion, clique, cult, whatever you'd call it."

"Distinctions such as these –"

"Such as what?

"Drawing distinctions such as these between religions and cults and cliques, it's always been dicey, and largely beside the point, I think. In any case, I now no longer believe what I once did."

"What was that?" the young man said.

"I used to believe it was largely a question of inter-pretation."

"But you no longer do?"

"I do not. Nor do I agree with the strict textbook or lexical criteria."

"What do you believe now?"

"That dogmatic conviction, which is a kind of faith, is at the root of it all. Whether the system in question is political, religious, artistic, quasi-artistic, dietary, economic, sexual, or anything else — including any cross-combinations, which they usually are — the belief in God or any other divine entity is beside the point."

They were both silent for several beats.

"When Kenneth was in the military," Hogan said, "he was a medic. He once saved the life of a Green Beret — a man who'd been shot in the chest. Kenneth not only expertly dressed the man's wound out in the field, but also carried this man for well over a hundred miles, over the course of days, deep in enemy territory. It was an act of extraordinary strength and heroism — truly the stuff of Congressional Medals of Honor. This man was forever after devoted to Kenneth. And yet for all Kenneth's undeniable intellectual power and his strength and his power to do good—in short, all his life-giving properties, and the thing inside him capable of such acts — I've always sensed that at the root of it all, something in him fundamentally worships at the shrine of death and violence."

Another long silence ensued.

The blood-orange moon wobbled up higher in the east, suffusing a small sector of sky with sulfurous light.

"As people do one thing," Hogan said, "so they do everything. This is what makes Kenneth difficult to comprehend. He is complex: capable of great violence and cruelty — I've seen it firsthand — but also great kindness. He genuinely mourns the loss of loved ones. I've seen that firsthand, as well. One thing is for certain, though."

"What is that?"

"A person's behavior, good or bad, bleeds through into any number of different areas."

"Bleeds through?"

"Yes," Hogan said. "It bleeds through."

19

DUSTY MAY DID NOT IMMEDIATELY MOVE. For a full hour, she stood like statuary in the center of the room. She stood thinking, ruminating.

What did it mean?

Was it an elaborate trick? A ploy to flush her out?

Or was it perhaps, after all, entirely in her head?

She looked down at the very real paper on the very real floor and she thought:

This is not all in my head.

She made a tight fold of her money and stuffed this into her front pocket. Careful as she was, quiet as she was, a quarter slipped out and rolled clattering across the wooden floor. She winced.

She slid open the rear window of her room and looked carefully up and down the streets, two stories below. There was no one to be seen. The streets loomed labyrinthian and misty. A deep silence hung over the city. The boulevards and alleyways seemed utterly deserted. But there were so many trees and shrubs and shadows and places where any person might easily hide.

Her black searching eyes flashed pony-like in the darkness.

"Come, Dusty May," she whispered to herself.

She strapped her backpack over her shoulders and cinched it, and then she slipped silently through the open window. She scaled down the cold wet metal ladder of the fire escape and dropped to the soundless street below.

She left the note unread upon the floor.

20

IMMEDIATELY UPON HITTING THE PAVEMENT, she darted off into the darkness of marginal backstreets. From here she began threading her way through a maze-like city she did not know. She made more turns than were necessary and even at several points doubled-back, as though to throw a hound off its scent: a maneuver characteristic of the hunted doe.

Above her, the clouds whirled away like cannon smoke, disclosing a full moon which shone down from the sky like a blind human eye — an eye bleeding through the fabric of the night. She could not decide if the full moon, which lighted her way but also exposed her, was good or bad for her plight.

The moon sliced the streets into intricate prisms of shadow and light.

She felt she could glide along through the darkness of the shadows on one side of the street, while at the same time keeping her eyes on the lighted sections across the way. Perhaps she did not pay enough attention to the dark side.

Yet she felt certain that at this moment no one was pursuing her.

She didn't know precisely where she was going, but in this moment she did not feel particularly overwhelmed: almost instinctively, she translated the shock of all her negative emotions into work and physical activity — her fundamental answer to everything now, after so many years of practice and self-discipline, the motions of her body in concert with her brain, her self-generated action wiping away all fears and incomprehensibility and the persistent sense of loneliness within her. Threading her way rapidly through the streets, she felt something greater, something not from without but from within, an invisible force, leading her forward.

Yet she had no precise plan. She was not even sure if all this was as she imagined. Wasn't everything a little too strange? She wanted no more strangeness in her life. One thing was certain: she was absolutely determined to uplift herself and to never go back to the house from which she'd escaped. She was like a vital animal who'd at last broken free from her cage, and now she sought a hole in which she might hide: a deep hole that did not terminate but went profoundly down and then rose back up, finally opening into a sunlit valley of fiery green grass and radiant fields of promise.

One hour later, the city still smoldering in leathery dark, she stopped walking at last.

As if by instinct, she turned around.

At that moment, she distinctly saw a black shape following her quite closely from the other side of the street. This figure was making every effort to keep itself concealed, staying deep within the shadows, but for a brief moment, the figure passed beneath a tangerine streetlight, and this is when she saw it. The shape quickly vanished back into the shadows.

"Come, Dusty May," she again whispered to herself.

She dropped down to the ground and slid under a parked pickup truck that sat silently in the moonlight. She moved like a spider beneath it.

She sprung up on the other side and then dashed into a narrow alleyway between two buildings, along the backside of which she circled around and went rapidly back in the approximate direction from which she'd just come. Here the street branched off at a sharp angle into a cul-de-sac, and this cul-de-sac is what she ran down, headlong.

21

AT THE END of the cul-de-sac, behind a row of private houses, a large park stretched away into the dark. This park contained tennis courts and basketball courts and a baseball diamond — and looming skeletally beyond, a steel lookout tower which rose four-hundred feet into the air. During the day, a caged elevator took people up to the top of this tower to an observation deck. Now, in the early morning, it stood mute and dimensionless against the purple sky.

Dusty darted between the private homes and over undulant lawns, and then she vaulted a low wooden fence that bordered the sleeping houses in all their ordered rows. At the border of the parkland, she realized that if she wanted get to the other side, there was no way to avoid exposing herself in that vast and lighted sprawl.

She stopped on the edge and for a moment looked back — beyond the fence over which she'd just leapt. She peered with her sharp eyes down the cul-de-sac behind her.

She saw no one.

A lumberyard glowed in the far distance. The moon in its circuit soared higher overhead. There was a small bicycle path that went anfractuously to her right and then dipped down into a lighted tunnel, and now she had to decide:

Should she go right, down the sinuous bicycle path into the light of the tunnel, or should she run through the wide-open space of the park?

She again looked to the right. She remembered from her map that on the other side of this tunnel was the train station — and there, she felt, lay safety.

She therefore started to turn this way, but the instant she did, she saw in the distant light of the tunnel what first looked to be a black statue. But it wasn't.

It was a man.

Who?

Who was it?

She did not know. She was startled. She looked back over her shoulder. There was no one behind her.

Had he been here all along, and was he unrelated to her pursuer?

Or had he just been posted here this moment, waiting for her, guarding the passageway to her safety?

She looked back to the moonlit park before her.

She didn't hesitate a second longer.

She sprinted as fast as she was able across the lighted space. It was a long way. She ran over gray stubble grass, a tiny figure in black tennis shoes gliding beneath the moonlight.

A quarter-mile later, on the other side of the open park, she found herself half-crouched among soft damp wood-chips that composed the ground upon which stood monkey-bars and teeter-totters and swing sets and a wide wavy slide. On her left, close enough for her to reach out and touch, a gigantic bullfrog of rubber sat beside a gigantic rubber tortoise, both waiting for little people to sit upon their backs.

She stood up straight, sweating and panting in the shadows beneath the slide. The ground felt spongy. Her breath came hard. The air was damp. She pushed her hair out of her eyes. Her shirt was soaked with sweat. All was silent but for her breath. She felt her shoulders slouch in fatigue from running so fast and so much, no sleep for far too long, her nerves stretched membrane-thin. She stood in the darkness of the playground and rested. Tiny tanagers in the tall trees beyond watched her with sesame eyes.

By and by, she peered out from under the slide and looked over the park she'd just run across. For a long moment she saw nothing. The park was deserted. The streets beyond were deserted. In fact, a full ten minutes passed, her breathing normalized, her fatigue fading, when suddenly the figure appeared.

It was forbidding in its black-clad presence, a club-like object in its hand, a long dark coat and round hat, a swift unswerving tread pounding through the darkness. The figure paused only a moment on the other side of the park, as if to get a more accurate bearing, and then it went energetically in the very direction Dusty May had come.

The black shape was now moving directly toward her.

She watched it.

She watched it come.

In that instant, under the full moon and the soaring lights of the park, the face of the figure shone perfectly, and she saw the horrifying visage of her former teacher and her foster father's fanatic friend: Wesson Weekly.

22

UNCERTAINTY WAS NOW GONE for Dusty May. It continued, however, for the man pursuing her, who still did not know precisely where she was — or what had suddenly come into her mind: a thing which gave her a glimmer of hope.

She took a deep breath.

The invisible force inside her pushed her toward the looming tower of steel. She made her way swiftly. Wesson Weekly first heard her, and then he spotted her.

He bolted after.

Dusty ran.

"Stop! Dusty May, stop!"

His voice was booming and unbelievably authoritative, as if it would halt her movement by its sheer volume and the weight and power of its authority — by this and this alone.

It had the opposite effect on her: she increased her speed and even in that moment thought of Kenneth Dvorak's words that life is movement.

She passed by a series of basketball courts whose free-throw lines glowed phosphorescent in the dark. She ran over the courts and through. She quickly came to the base of the towering structure and saw a sign that said:

CLOSED FOR RENOVATIONS

Still running, she circled the entire perimeter of the tower. Madly she scanned the structure for a ladder. She could see the black shape moving toward her with a terrifying sense of purpose. She found a ladder at last. It began twelve feet above her head, far higher than she could ever leap. But this did not prevent her from moving up the metal skeleton.

With trembling fingers, she cinched her backpack more securely around her ribcage. She made sure her money was pushed deep down into the pointy tip of her front pocket. With both hands, she clutched the great sweep of metal that arced enormously from the ground, forming one claw of the tower's base. Then, slung underneath it upside-down, like an orangutan, she began moving upward, hand over hand, inching toward the ladder. The metal was flat and cold. From this vantage, she saw all the way up through the naked beams, up to the pinnacle of the tower, which was sunk in cottony mist.

Out of the corner of her eye, to the left and slightly below her, below the long arcing foot she was scaling, she caught movement: the black shape pounding toward her more vigorously still. She looked back up through the naked steel in a kind of despair.

She climbed faster.

When she got to the ladder, Weekly was directly below. He was running with the long club in hand, his hat long flown away, and now he leapt with all his might. She was still upside-down. He grunted loudly — a low and beastlike moan — and as he leapt, he swung the club at her head.

It missed.

She thought she heard it swish past, imagined she felt wind from its force pass over her — and in that moment she understood explicitly what until now she'd only suspected:

This man sought not to capture but kill her.

The heavy wooden club clattered against the metal. Weekly landed on his knees and sprung up instantly. He threw off his coat and, leaving the club on the ground, began scaling the base of the tower.

Spider-like, Dusty went up. She knew there was no going back now — not ever — and gazing upward, she felt as though she were climbing into the misty heavens of the unknown, where eagles rode the thermals and molten meteorites rocketed down through the stratosphere, burning out into smoking spalls of cosmic slag.

She was not afraid of heights.

She knew her pursuer was.

The ladder was wet and slick. She climbed on. She climbed cautiously, yet she was quick and strong. From below, she was scarcely visible in her dark clothes. Such a quietly moving person who even in such a state made hardly any sound at all. Between her feet, she could see him below her. Unlike her, he was totally unencumbered — no jacket, no backpack — and still he moved with much less certainty than she did. He labored. Yet he, too, was very agile and strong. The muscle striations in his forearms stood out like metal grooves. He reached the ladder when she was approximately halfway to the top of the tower. Here he began a straight upward pursuit, after her.

23

THE FIRST KERNEL of daylight grew in the east and then spread out across the August sky, nullifying the morning stars one by one. The mist blew away. The sky overhead went leaden and gray.

Below her, moving slower the higher he climbed, Wes Weekly struggled upward. Vertigo rocked him like a club-blow. His stomach surged.

Dusty continued her ascent. When she came to the top of the tower, the whole eastern sky was alight and pulsing, a strange cabbage-green, the last stars gleaming like snake eyes inside the celadon vault. Cars were beginning to crawl along the highways far below. She stood atop the metal platform. She stood completely exposed. She held onto the rail and looked down. The baseball diamond looked pristine and toy-like so distant beneath her feet. A small wind blew over her. It lifted her Indian-black hair. Her skin was the color of toffee. South of the tower, on the edge of the park, a string of pearly ponds lay smoking like pools of hot milk, or mercury, the river beyond slow and level: laid across the land like a blade.

The metal platform was fenced off and under construction. A long I-beam cantilevered some fifty feet out into high open space. It stood perfectly horizontal and went almost to the top of a construction crane, the huge white mast of which lay angled dramatically across the arced and empty sky.

Dusty produced a small cylindrical object from the inside of her coat pocket. She looked down. She realized only now how much slower her pursuer was coming — slower, it seemed, with each rung. And yet he was still climbing, still coming — coming for her — and she knew he would not stop.

She drew back from the hole through which the ladder penetrated the platform. She waited. She looked again at the I-beam jutting out into space. It was perhaps one foot wide. She got down onto her knees and sat on the back of her feet.

She could see him clearly through the metal mesh of the platform. She watched him come. Her black eyes contained no emotion but sat in their sockets like dark slots.

When, at last, her wolfish pursuer was near the top, she leaned over and peered straight down at him through the circular ladder-hole. He heard her movement above, and he gazed upward. His face was beet-red, agleam with sweat. His nostrils looked like auger holes, his crazy eyes charged with suffering. He was devastated by his fear of heights, and yet he was climbing higher still. Suddenly he grunted. She did not know why, but the sound of it went through her with a horrible chill. He was very close now. She moved with great celerity.

Extreme situations can produce flashes of lightning, which sometimes blind and sometimes illuminate. Weekly's wild gaze saw what was about to happen — but he saw it a fraction too late.

Dusty brought forth the cylindrical object in her hand and in the same motion she released its contents down onto his upturned face.

It was mace.

She gassed him fully in his eyes. He grunted again and screamed more loudly still. He shut his eyes and buried his chin into his chest. He clung desperately to the ladder, draping his right arm through the rung and holding it with the crook of his elbow. She sprayed more mace onto him, showering his head with toxic rain, and she kept spraying until the can was empty.

Weekly clung to the ladder and held his breath. The cool breeze blew. She watched him. She watched him do the unthinkable:

He continued climbing up toward her.

She threw the empty can of mace at him, striking him on the crown of his head, but for all the force with which she threw it, the empty can was not heavy or solid enough to do damage.

It bounced off his misshapen skull with an ice-like tink and then went cartwheeling through space to the ground below.

His right hand reached for the top rung. His eyes, barely open, wept hot chemical tears. She saw his sandy-colored hair blowing in the breeze. She sat down on the platform and with both feet, she stomped on his head. She did it again. With a swift backhanded motion of his right arm, his left hand still holding with an iron-grip to the ladder, he swiped purblind for her — and caught her left foot under his arm.

She felt his great strength, saw the cannonball of his

biceps swell beneath his tee-shirt sleeve. He clutched her foot against his body, held it in his armpit, and simultaneously he twisted his torso in such a way that it seemed to her at all once that he'd pull them both off the tower together if he could, sending them tumbling to their deaths as one.

She jerked back with such force that it astonished him. She broke free and with the energy of ultimate struggle, she jumped to her feet and bound across the small platform — and without any hesitation, she leapt the metal fence that enclosed the observation deck.

She walked out onto the I-beam which stretched fifty feet away into open space, toward the mast of the crane.

They act swiftly who are in ultimate clash with their destiny.

24

THE GROUND LOOMED four-hundred feet below her. Yet for a moment, stepping onto the beam, she felt herself almost uplifted, and as though she were moving across pure air itself.

Before she had time to think, she was ten feet away from the observation deck, walking the beam which was damp with morning dew, both arms stretched out horizontal for balance, and from below, she looked a black cruciform figure, graceful and otherworldly against the nacre heavens.

It was then that she heard another loud moan behind her.

She did not look back.

She stepped carefully but did not inch or creep: one foot in front of the other, a small slip of her tennis shoe on the dew-moist metal, which sent her heart into her throat, but still walking, still moving forward — a very wide balance beam indeed, she told herself — while the breeze came harder, pouring over and under her like water without any sound, and then a gust of wind that went wildly about her hair, blowing black strands everywhere across her face, and her black eyes watered, and all the open sky swarming around her in a vertiginous swirl, and still she kept walking farther out into space.

When she was at last near the other end of the beam, she felt the thick metal shudder beneath her. Then she heard a dull bong which sent sound vibrations up through her feet and into her legs and pelvis. Still, she did not look back.

She came to the end of the beam and knew that this was the hardest part of all: two feet away to the top of the crane mast.

She sat with great care on the edge of the beam. Her legs dangled below her. She touched the mast with the tip of her tennis shoe. It was solid. She clutched each side of the metal, cold beneath her grip, her small dark hands white now from the strength of her clutch, and only at this time did she allow herself to glance back over her shoulder.

What she saw shocked her:

Wesson Weekly, who had first tried to shake the beam but found it too solid to budge, was now flat on his stomach partway out on the beam but locked there, motionless, completely paralyzed with acrophobic panic. He clung to the beam in a giant bear-hug, his eyes squished shut, and he could no longer move at all, not forward or backward.

She saw his face turn ashen and then paper-white. These heights were too great for him. She turned back to the crane mast. She reached out with her hand. To her overwhelming relief, she found she was almost able to touch the top of the mast, though not quite.

Yet it was again with the unhesitating energy of ultimate struggle which her body contained that Dusty May inhaled once deeply and then, in a reckless instant of life or death, she pushed herself, half leaping from her rear, toward the iron-lace of the crane. Unmoored for a fraction of a moment in empty space, she floated and clutched madly at the soaring mast.

She caught it.

The metal smacked her face with force, but she was safe.

She hugged the cold crane and then she got her feet under her. She looked back to the beam she'd just walked. She saw her pursuer still paralyzed in the exact same spot, but he was open-eyed now, raddle-eyed, wild, still weeping mace, grunting and screaming and moaning, watching her as if he would bring her down with the tractor-beam of his gaze alone.

Their eyes met and locked.

His face was plastered with saliva. His nose bled. She held his fear-crazed stare for a full ten seconds, and then she began climbing down the crane.

Seconds later, something — perhaps another moan of hatred — made her look back.

What she saw next shook and astounded her forever after.

She saw Wesson Weekly deliberately push himself off the edge of the beam and fall to his death.

She watched him sail soundlessly into the silver void below, dropping down through cold empty space, almost serenely turning through the air — no more animal cries now but silent as a martyr — before bursting in an explosion of blood and gore onto the ungiving earth.

PART III

25

SHE DRIFTED south into the baked desert country of Arizona: sun-struck little villages where the foehn wind blew dry and hot down the leeward side of the White Mountains, and lenticular clouds hovered in the sky like alien saucers. It was important for her in these days to keep moving.

She grew quickly to love the hot wind and the heat and the desert. She ate little, drank a great deal of water. She slept in hostels, YWCA's, roadside motels, all-night laundromats. She spent hours staring at the nighttime sky strewn utterly with emerald stars. Her money meanwhile dribbled away. Her situation grew grave. She was sixteen-years-old.

In Phoenix, she discovered she could make instant cash doing front flips and backflips. People would give five or ten or even twenty dollars to watch her do these flips off the ungiving pavement, so that in one week's time, she had more money in her pocket than when she'd left home.

One afternoon two weeks after she'd watched Wesson Weekly plummet to his death, at a park where martial artists, gymnasts, parkourists, body-builders, and other elite athletes exercised and competed, she bet a group of massive

men over half of all she had that she could do more consecutive pull-ups than any one of them, and this bet was
quickly accepted by the fittest.

It was a warm windless day. She produced five crisp one-
hundred dollar bills for everyone to see. Three days in a row
now, she'd observed from afar the athletes at this park, and
she felt sure of her skill and strength matched against theirs.

That man laughed in a slow friendly way who accepted
before any of the others, and all the others laughed as well
— at first.

Her challenger was twenty-four-years-old, shirtless,
blue-eyed, bald, with a fine-shaped skull, cafe-au-lait skin,
and long lean muscles: lats like an hourglass, wasp-waisted,
mutant abdominals.

A young lady came over to Dusty and, speaking softly in
her ear, advised her against challenging this particular man.

"Why?" Dusty said.

"He's the strongest and he's the best," the young lady
said. "He's famous."

Dusty didn't say anything, but shook her head to indi-
cate that she didn't care about any of this.

They flipped a coin to determine who would go first, and
Dusty May lost the toss.

The young man introduced himself:

"My name is Jason." He smiled. His teeth were very
white. She thought him handsome.

"My name is Dusty."

"Nice to meet you, Dusty. I'll go first."

She nodded. "Wide-grip," she said. "And they must be
real pull-ups — clean pull-ups: all the way past the chin, all
the way down to full-arm extension, but no pausing or
resting at the top or the bottom. Do you agree?"

Jason laughed again, and so did the others.

"Of course," Jason said.

By now, a large group of people had gathered around. Many wondered if this was a practical joke of some sort, and several looked for hidden cameras.

Jason designated one man from among the group to count. This man wore a gray baseball cap, which he now turned backwards. Jason chalked-up his hands and clapped his palms together, sending a miniature explosion of chalk-dust into the xeric air. He gripped the pull-up bar and began.

He was practiced and exceptionally strong. He wasn't entirely used to extending all the way down, without a slight crook at the elbows, yet his form was perfect. He had virtually no fat anywhere on his body. His wide back squirmed with muscles.

Dusty watched him.

The counter barked out each number loudly and clearly.

"One. Two. Three. Four. Five ..."

Jason had his legs crossed at the ankles, tucked up at about a forty-five degree angle. The soles of his sneakers were red and had arrowhead-shaped treads, and there were grass blades stuck to them. Dusty's black eyes took in everything but were emotionless. She wore pleated khaki shorts and a light beige tee-shirt with half sleeves. Her arms were very thin and extraordinarily dark — almost black — from her recent exposure to the desert sunlight. The crowd had grown larger and everyone except the counter was silent.

Jason started to visibly tire at twenty-three pull-ups. His finely shaped skull glistered with perspiration, and the sun reflected off his head in a diamond-shaped pattern. He kept going. His back tapered specimen-like into his waist.

At thirty-three pull-ups, he grew a little shaky.

At thirty-eight, his form went more sloppy still, yet he managed eight more after that, all of which were just passable, and then he dropped lightly to the ground. He was breathing hard. The wormy veins that ran down each of his biceps stood engorged and throbbing.

The onlookers clapped.

He turned around. Somebody threw him a white cloth, and he toweled off his face and his bald head, and then he nodded to Dusty.

"It makes a huge difference when you must go all the way up and all the way down," she said. She was not speaking in any way condescendingly but in total commiseration for the difficulty of the task.

Jason nodded once but didn't reply. He was still winded.

Dusty tied back her long black hair, which was like the hair of a Japanese girl. Jason offered her his bag of chalk. She accepted in silence, her lips parting slightly in a smile, revealing the dark gap between her two front teeth. She chalked her hands and then stood underneath the pull-up bar. She was not nearly tall enough to reach it. The ground beneath her was grassy. The whiteness of the chalk made the darkness of her skin more emphatic. She took a deep breath.

A great many people were gathered around now to watch this impromptu contest of strength, a number of whom, however, were still questioning whether it was real or a practical joke. Some of the onlookers murmured. All eyes were upon her.

Abruptly, then, like a panther, Dusty May sprung up to the bluish bar. She hung for a split second. Then she adjusted her grip and began.

She cranked out pull-ups like a machine, her motions so fluid, so deft. She pumped them out. She was methodical and crisp. She went all the way up and all the way down. The counter was counting faster for her than he had for Jason.

When she got to twenty-five, it was clear to everybody that this was no joke.

When she got to thirty, she'd still not visibly slowed.

When she got to thirty-five, everybody grew strangely hushed. When she got to forty, it was clear to all that she would win. When she got to fifty, it looked as though she might still have more in her.

She dropped from the bar and turned to Jason — who did not have five-hundred dollars.

26

DUSTY MAY WAS NOT QUITE SO naive, and the truth was she didn't expect he'd be able to pay. In fact, she had other designs.

She went to Jason, who was eating from a large bag of purple jellybeans and discussing money-matters with a loud-voiced human on the other end of his phone. He saw Dusty and disconnected. Dusty led him off to the side, away from the onlookers. She spoke to him at length, not in a whisper but in a voice so soft that no one heard her except him. He was facing forward as she spoke, his profile turned toward her. He was still eating blueberry jellybeans, one at a time, chewing speculatively. He scowled the entire time, nodded twice, replied once, appeared to be listening with great interest.

In the end, he turned and faced her and Dusty extracted from her front pocket the five one-hundred dollar bills. She gave him the money and something else as well. After that, it was agreed they would meet later that night at this very location.

When they were finished speaking, Dusty went back to

the jungle-gym. The crowd had largely dispersed. A few onlookers were still milling around, many of whom were eyeing her. She had no awareness of them. Her concentration was suddenly one-pointed. She sprung and in the same motion muscled-up to the highest bar on the jungle-gym.

The remaining onlookers grew captivated.

In the blink of an eye — so quickly, in fact, that everyone observing her felt they'd missed a step — she was on her feet and walking tightrope-style in her black sneakers along the thin circular bar that went around the jungle-gym. The grassy ground loomed nine feet below. The pull-up bar upon which she'd just done fifty consecutive pull-ups stood seven feet to her left. Everyone stopped talking. They watched her with upcast eyes. None watched her as closely as Jason.

Lightly, she made her way around. Her arms were outstretched and horizontal: a lithe and cruciate shape, maintaining gracefully her precarious balance. She walked carefully but quickly, still unaware of all eyes upon her. There was an unassailable, immutable expression of focus stamped upon her face — a look that was totally unselfconscious, and which made a lasting impression on every single person who saw her.

She completed a full circuit of the jungle-gym and then she stopped. She wobbled slightly and turned a quarter turn. From here, she leapt seven feet across to the pull-up bar. She sailed through the air. She caught the bar, and in the same motion, she began swinging.

She swung once, twice, and then she went into a giant swing, full rotation, her body completely extended, and she continued swinging in this way around and around the pull-up bar. Her feet easily cleared the ground. She increased her speed. Her hair was still tied back, flying behind her. There was a conspicuous lightness in her body, an overwhelming sense of energy. She was rotating so fast that it seemed to many that something must soon give.

Suddenly, silently, she released the bar with her left hand and made two full one-armed giant swings at break-neck speed. It was an act of great strength and great danger.

Still swinging, then, she reached back to the pull-up bar with her left hand and again gripped it with both, and in a sort of full-bodied tuck-and-release motion, gaining more momentum yet, she cranked around the bar faster still, so that the entire metal apparatus jostled and creaked. She spun around once, twice — and then, just before releasing, two things happened simultaneously:

She felt deep within her body a subtle but unmistakable tremor, as if some force had struck her bone at a profound depth with a single blow of hammer-and-chisel — and at that exact moment also, the image of her foster father appeared before her, but distantly and as if entirely real: like a man viewed through the wrong end of a telescope, distinct and perfectly clear, but somehow rendered very small.

All this happened in a flash which lasted less than half a beat.

She released and in midair tucked herself into an unbelievably fast backflip and then came out of it and landed on the grass — a perfect landing but for a slight twist of her left ankle, which did not hurt much, and yet it felt to her strangely ominous.

Everyone around her broke out in applause and shrill whistling. Jason narrowed his eyes on her, then dropped his gaze to the ground. He seemed all at once melancholy.

An enormous and steroidal-looking black man, who was stripped to the waist and had globe-like shoulders, an eight-pack, and pectorals that drooped, came over to her and spoke.

"Little girl," he said. "You." He paused. "You an absolute beast."

Dusty's lips broke slightly into a gap-toothed smile.

The massive man gave her little hand a high-five.

27

WHAT DUSTY SOUGHT WAS a new identity: a new passport with a spurious name, a new social-security card. Jason told her that he could provide this, and she told him she would pay another five-hundred upon receipt.

She knew she was taking a large risk.

But it was a risk the potential consequences and reward for which she'd methodically measured and weighed — well before she ever posed a pull-up challenge. So that when, later that night, she came to the park with her black backpack on her back and a large bag of blueberry jelly-beans tucked under her arm as a gift for him, and she found neither him nor anyone else there, she felt herself inwardly deflate with disappointment. Yet she was not altogether surprised.

She waited for one hour, which turned into two. From a granite plinth, some twenty feet to her left, a marble Mother-of-God, shawled in black moss, watched Dusty with stone eyes. The night air was warm and gentle, but a smell of dust and something almost meaty laced the air. Crickets in the shrubbery strummed low chords. The breeze blew in and lifted her hair as with tiny fingers. The crescent moon hung in the west like an earring made of hammered gold.

Near midnight, when she turned to leave, she was half-startled to see a middle-aged man sitting alone on a park bench behind her in the dark.

Had he been there this entire time?

She did not know.

She regarded him for a moment and he regarded her. He had a serene and non-hostile presence. He continued to sit. He nodded to her when he saw her notice him.

"Good evening," he said.

His voice was soft. His hair glowed whitely from within the shadows of the trees among which he sat, a thick forelock dangling over his left eye.

Dusty nodded in return but did not speak. She'd suddenly become faintheaded and a little dizzy. She started to leave but the man spoke again.

"Be alert and watchful of your steps," he said. "You're a sheep among wolves."

She shook her head and scowled. What was that? The New Testament? Some wandered biblical zealot stumbled into these precincts to admonish her from the outer darkness of the park?

Yet something in his voice sounded terribly heartfelt, premonitory even. She hurried on. At the edge of the park, she threw the bag of blueberry jellybeans violently into the maw of a trashcan.

One block later, sweating and more faintheaded still, walking so swiftly that she was almost running, she glanced up and over to her left, and at first she saw no one. Still, something made her stop and look longer. She felt a sudden sense of apprehension rising within her. She sweated inordinately now, though not from heat. An intermittent barb of pain yanked like a fishhook behind her right eyeball. After a moment, she observed in the middle-distance a black car glide up to the curb and stop. Her vision blurred, then sharpened. She felt herself totter. Sweat beaded on her forehead and stood there like blisters.

She blinked slowly. When she opened her eyes, she saw the vast corpus of her foster father emerge from the car. He was dressed in a black suit-and-tie, his great bald dome glowing lunar-like under the glaucous lights of a theater marquis.

Kenneth Dvorak turned and looked at her, as if he'd known all along precisely where she was.

She bolted.

28

A<small>T ALMOST THIS</small> exact same time, when Dusty was across the park and one block removed, the middle-aged man in the shadows, who knew nothing at that moment of Dusty's plight, rose from the bench and went in the opposite direction from her. His walk and movements were not hurried.

He walked across the grass to the dust-strewn street where his motorcycle sat gleaming on its kickstand. He was a large and imposing man. His name was Hogan Phillips. He produced from his back pocket a pair of gray gloves, and he tugged them on. He kickstarted his bike and drove eastward, out of the city, on a small highway. He cruised along at an easy fifty miles per hour. Traffic was desultory. He wore no helmet. The cyclopean eye of his headlight swept conically through the darkness. The desert wind went wildly about his hair. The horizon to the west was a long band of lemon-yellow light which looked as if at the edge of the earth some strange vegetable matter were being slowly compressed out of existence.

He soon came to a small diner burning in the Arizona night. He parked his motorcycle and tilted it onto its kickstand and then went inside the diner. He took off his gloves and stuffed them into his back pocket. He was met by a young man in faded jeans and a white tee-shirt.

They shook hands. The young man invited him to the counter. They both ordered coffee and iced water. The waitress wore a white cotton dress with red stripes, like a candy cane, and her hair was the color of candied yams. She was curvy and good-looking. The two men sat in the diner and talked. Outside, the golden moon rode the oceanic heavens like a sky canoe, and the desert wind seethed softly through the sand. The two men talked for some time.

At length, they both rose from the counter and the young man put a twenty dollar bill on the countertop. They went outside and stood in the parking lot. The young man was not nearly as tall as the older man. They exchanged a few more words and then they shook hands again.

After that, they went their separate ways.

29

DUSTY RAN AS FAST as her legs would carry her, striving to put as much distance as possible between herself and Kenneth Dvorak. For a long time she did not slow her pace at all, nor did she look back.

She pounded down neighborhood lanes and through alleys and residential side-streets and over silent lawns. She pounded down the labyrinthian ways.

She pounded on and she did not stop — until, at last, along the raggedy edge of the desert, where the asphalt gave way to sand and up ahead the railroad tracks began, she stepped on something that went through the thin sole of her sneaker and punctured the heal of her left foot.

She gasped.

She stopped running.

She swung around and saw that she was all alone in the towering night.

She saw also that what she'd stepped on was a long thick nail sticking through an old piece of wood. Her blood shone purple all along the nail-shaft. It was here, hobbling and migrainous, soaked in sweat and still pouring down more, she began to question whether or not she'd seen her foster father after all.

The dry wind sprung up and gusted. It blew stinging particles of sand across her face. She squished her eyes shut and turned her back to the wind. The sand blasted her. She crouched on her haunches. The wind blew harder. Her long hair thrashed over her face. The moon was down. Soon all the dark air about her was hung with a thick pall of desert dust, and the cherry-and-apricot lights of the city beyond lay dimly upcast on the sky, like a bomb blast. The wind continued to blow.

Her punctured foot throbbed in unison with her heartbeat and her head. She felt little creatures crawling everywhere inside her, infiltrating her, hammering away deep down: hammering at the cells that made up her tissue and her bones and her muscles and her essence.

She was bleeding through her sock.

She was bleeding through.

She crouched upon the desert floor in the lonely howling wind, and she crouched there in silence, wounded and completely alone.

PART IV

30

It was the first week of September and a tide had overtaken the coastal town. Water lay gently sloshing through the streets. She arrived at twilight in the rain.

Through the window of the bus, she saw a banner-sign stretched pole-to-pole across Main Street — a banner advertising a traveling circus — and she saw also that the circus had been cancelled because of weather. Her insides liquefied.

The marine air hung thick with the smell of salt and fish. She'd been sitting so long that when at last she stood up to disembark from the bus, she was stunned into disorientation by the bloodbeat of pain that smashed through her injured foot. She looked down.

To her astonishment, she saw that her wound had bled clear through the black fabric of her tennis shoe. She stared at it until her vision grew blurry.

Stepping off the bus and onto solid ground, the planet seemed to wobble beneath her feet, and she knew beyond any doubt now that what she secretly feared had come to pass: she'd not be doing backflips or front flips any time soon.

She had no credit cards, no bank account, and her money was running out.

In the course of the long bus ride, she'd seen her foster father twice: the first time, he was standing dreamlike along the shoulder of a windswept highway among tall swaying grass, tractor roads curving off into the intricate horizon. The second time, he was in the passenger's seat of a long black car gliding past the Greyhound.

Both times, he was looking directly at her.

In the bathroom stall of the bus depot, door locked, alone among the astringent odors of spearmint and urine and the soft crackle of water, she emptied her pockets onto her backpack, and here she discovered that she had just about enough money left to pay for a doctor's visit.

Not one hour later, at a walk-in clinic, Dusty May sat begowned on the edge of the doctor's table. The nurse who checked her in, noting in silence Dusty's cold sweat and her white-hot fever, had first given her a tetanus shot and then something for the pain. The pain medication was already taking hold.

"Won't it just go away?" Dusty said to the doctor now. "Won't it heal on its own?"

"If you ignore the wound, you mean?" the doctor said.

"Yes."

"No." The doctor paused. His green eyes swam like exotic fish behind his octagonal glasses. His silver hair was slicked strait back, with wide comb-tracks like furrows, his pumpkin-colored scalp visible beneath. "Or, rather, it depends," he said.

"On what?"

"On how deep down your wound goes, and if there was nerve damage, which I think there was."

"Can you tell by looking at it how deep down it goes?" she said.

"Not precisely. But I can see that it goes pretty deep. Also, I believe other factors have been introduced which have compounded the initial injury."

"What do you mean?"

"Other parts of your foot have been affected — including, as I say, the nerves."

"How many problems do I have now?"

"It's difficult to say. But those other problems, too, have potential offshoots."

A momentary silence fell.

"What happens if it doesn't?" she said.

"Doesn't what?"

"Heal properly."

"It will fester."

"For how long?"

The doctor seemed for a moment puzzled by the question.

"For life, possibly," he said.

Dusty didn't respond.

"Very often," the doctor continued, "these sorts of injuries will heal on the surface but get infected underneath. Think of your wound in the shape of a funnel, which yours actually is. The word for that, if you're interested, is infundibular. You have an infundibular puncture wound, Dusty May."

Here he smiled at her, and his smile eased her anxiety, so that her lips as well opened up, revealing the gap between her two front teeth.

"Infundibular," she repeated to herself.

"The proper and healthy way for a wound to heal is from the bottom up" — the doctor gestured with both hands, stacking one atop the other — "beginning deep down at the tip of the funnel and gradually rising to the top, as though you're carefully filling the funnel with a mending mud."

He paused again.

"Can you picture this?" he said.

Dusty nodded.

"If the wound is superficial," he said, "or fairly superficial, as most wounds are, ignoring it won't cause any real problems or scarring or lasting damage."

"But?" she said.

"But?" he said. "There is no but."

"I'm sorry. I thought I heard hesitation," she said.

"No, no hesitation. None whatsoever. As I said, if the wound is very deep, ignoring it will greatly exacerbate things."

"It will fester," she said.

"Yes."

"But it will go away — *eventually?*" she said. "My body will heal."

"No, not necessarily. It might. But it could also become chronic — especially if there's nerve damage."

"What if I move to a different climate — a healthier climate?"

"Your injury will follow you."

She didn't respond. She pictured and then felt an army of little creatures like bugs infiltrating her, marching all throughout her body, chipping away at her.

"In fact," he said, "the deeper down it goes, the more nerve damage it can cause if you ignore it — all the more if there are still other factors yet introduced. Then those other factors could become primary."

"What do you mean?"

"I mean that 'festering' hardly describes it."

"You describe it," she said. "I want you to describe it."

"It can create a kind of chain reaction within you, so that the integrity of your foot and then your nervous system and your entire body are breached." The doctor paused. He watched her. "The human body is completely interconnected," he said, "the nervous system in particular, which is electric. And so if you ignore a serious injury, it can ramify all throughout you."

She again felt little bug-like creatures invading her, saw black insects hopping along the margins of her vision, which when she turned to look at them directly were not there.

She stared back into the doctor's magnified eyes that were so kind and gentle.

"You must not ignore your injuries, Dusty May. You must heal them. Understand that. Understand, too, that human health and human happiness are deeply interwoven and interconnected, and they are not a cause but an effect — a by-product."

"What do you mean?"

"I mean they must ensue."

31

Dusty May stood upon an ancient-looking cobblestone quay watching the slate-blue swells suck and heave. Soot-colored seagulls wheeled shrieking through the windy air. Flights of pelicans deploying downwind. Water lay everywhere. She'd never seen so much of it.

Her foot felt much better from the antibiotics and the shot and the ointment the doctor had given her, and upon which she'd spent all but the last of her money. The doctor had then told her to rest awhile, and he'd pulled the door shut as he left the room. It was a gesture of kindness for which she was very grateful. When she'd awakened at last, she had no idea how much time had elapsed. The doctor had left her alone and totally undisturbed in the room. She woke and gathered up her backpack and slipped out in silence.

Now in spite of how dire her situation had become, in spite of the desolate sensation swelling inside her, she felt a certain buoyancy in sloshing through the salty water, which ran loosely through the streets. The cold water and the salt within it was good for her injury, the cold anesthetizing her foot. The water saturated her shoes, the spanking wavelets breaking over her shins. Childhood memories swamped her: memories of splashing alone through rainy puddles in her red fireman boots, under low leaden Nevada skies; the mealy odor of wet autumn leaves, feathers of mist, the wreckage of leaves pitched like rib-cages in the grass.

She was very hungry now and tired, and she knew that she'd eventually have to eat and sleep and that this would require the very last of her money. But for this moment she didn't let herself think about any of it.

She waded out across cobblestones up to her knees in cold water. Her backpack was cinched securely upon her back. There, atop a wrack of rubbery kelp, she found what looked to be a small telescope made for a child.

She extracted it from the kelp and held it up to her right eye, her left eye squished shut. She pointed it toward the thin blue pencil-line of the horizon, where the sea merged with the sky.

Immediately she saw that it was not a telescope at all but a kaleidoscope.

Contained within its cryptic tube was a kind of blurry arcana which, in a matter of moments, clarified before her eye, so that suddenly she saw inside of it a multitude of tiny men — tiny but distinct, as something viewed through the wrong end of binoculars — and then she saw that these multiplying miniature men were the same man, and that this man was her foster father Kenneth Dvorak.

An icicle skewered her heart. Her scalp numbed. Simultaneously, she understood what was happening and why she'd been seeing him everywhere. She dropped the kaleidoscope to her side, and in a state of horror she thought:

He's infiltrated me.

With dread rising like cold water inside her, she turned

quickly away and walked in the other direction of the quay, where she was again swamped by childhood memories: a miniature sailboat with a little tin anchor floating by her feet in the sluicing street. She watched it drift past. When it was gone, she felt herself hesitant to look up — frightened that she'd perhaps see her shadow-self as a very young child: ankle-deep in the water and staring back at her in stony silence.

But when she lifted her eyes, she saw no one at all.

She gazed forlornly at the watery streets and the alien village and the low slate sky.

The sloshing sound of the water soothed her.

She debated whether she should keep the kaleidoscope and the terrible things it contained, and then she made a decision:

She threw it shattering into the nearest wastebasket.

She continued walking.

She came upon a narrow canal, the water of which was almost still — curiously still, she thought. The cry of seagulls was like the sound of nails being pulled from wet wood. A set of old granite steps, blotched with blue lichen, rose from the water into a resting place, a sort of walkway stretching above the streets and which was comparatively dry. She mounted these steps and then sat down on the top one. She pulled her knees into her midsection. Her foot pulsed faintly, but it felt far better than it had at any other time since the injury. She looked about. She realized only now that she'd lost track of where she was. It seemed a residential section near the purlieus of the town.

She felt disoriented and grew acutely aware of how little money she had and how dire her situation.

She stared at the indigo water so motionless below her, a diagonal of the silver sky angled across the water's face, reflected seabirds skating through. As she was staring at it, she thought she heard the clop of footsteps coming up behind her. She turned.

It was a man epicene and inordinately good-looking, early thirties, perhaps, short and thin and somehow doll-like in his perfect features, dressed in black slacks with blade-like creases and a white button-down shirt, the sleeves of which were folded once off his narrow wrists. He had curly blonde hair that hung in ringlets. He was wearing round sunglasses, and when she looked at him, she saw her dark face replicated minutely in each lens. The man stopped before her and extended to her a white envelope.

He did not speak. His polished shoes gleamed like glass.

Dusty rose to her feet. She hesitated. Then she took the envelope from the man and slit it open with her pinky.

Inside were five crisp one-hundred dollar bills and the passport she'd given Jason.

When she opened up the passport, she saw that her photo was the exact same, but her name had been changed: Lucy Gray.

She wondered for a moment if she were dreaming. Then, rapidly, she stuffed everything back into the envelope and pushed it safely down into her front pocket.

"Can I be of any help?" the man said to her.

"I don't know," Dusty said.

"He wanted me to tell you that he was sorry."

Dusty's heart skipped a beat. "Who?" she said. "Who did?"

"Jason. It was a far more difficult job than he'd anticipated."

Dusty released the breath she'd unconsciously been holding. She didn't say anything. Her black eyes went back to the motionless water of the canal, where their reflected figures floated like shadows. She thought of Jason. Then she turned back to the man before her.

He extended his hand. "I'm Andrew."

His fingers were elegant and they felt warm and pleasant against her cold wet flesh. In that moment, he seemed to Dusty almost uncanny in his neatness and his cleanliness. A vampiric palpation.

"I'm Dusty."

"You're soaked."

"I was sloshing through the water."

"May I buy you a cup of coffee?"

"You may."

32

"HOW DID YOU FIND ME?" she said.

They were sitting at the counter of a small coffeeshop, not far from where he'd approached her, a second-story cafe with thick glass windows that commanded a full view of the heaving ocean. Far off, the black-and-white flash of a killer whale. The air outside was turning blue, the village shadowy and silent. She sipped the scalding coffee carefully and with great satisfaction. Two little brown-haired young women, both clad in black, sat at a table by one of the windows. A solitary man was reading a book in the booth adjacent.

"Purely by chance," Andrew said. "One of Jason's friends saw you getting on the bus."

Andrew had taken off his sunglasses now, and she saw that his eyes were piercing and gray.

Dusty took another sip of coffee. She still had her backpack on her back, and she dimly thought that she'd be more comfortable if she took it off. But in the end, she decided not to bother.

"Why didn't he keep the money?" she said.

Andrew was silent for several beats. She watched him. He really was exceptionally fine-featured, she thought again, so doll-like and diminutive, his blonde hair hanging in perfect spirals like double-helix.

"Because he didn't deliver on time." Andrew paused. "And because he admires you."

Dusty dropped her eyes. For a fleeting instant, she thought she smelled Kenneth Dvorak's aftershave drifting by.

"Why did you buy a bus ticket to this place specifically?" Andrew said.

"Because," Dusty answered swiftly, "there's a –"

But here she broke off. Something had suddenly occurred to her, something that struck her like a thunder-clap. She looked at Andrew, who was smiling serenely, so doll-like, so pristine, his eyelashes long and dark and beating slowly, like the wings of a strange bird.

"Yes?" he said. "Because there's a ... what?"

"A beautiful ocean strand that my foster mother — that my mother and I once visited when I was very little."

She sipped her coffee. Her sharp mind was racing, grasping, apprehending, formulating, her dark eyes dilated with conjecture — and then something else:

The solitary man reading in the booth stood up to leave. He strode past and when he pushed open the front door, for a brief but seminal moment, Dusty saw outside. What she saw was a large dark-skinned man with a white forelock, who was standing not far from the cafe. Then the door shut.

It took Dusty only a moment, and she remembered.

She was inwardly thankful that she'd not taken off her backpack.

"This coffee is delicious," she said.

"I agree," Andrew said.

"It's revivified me."

"Revivified?"

"Yes. Very much. I must now use the restroom."

"It's that way, I believe." Andrew gestured to the right with his porcelain chin, a divot embedded deeply within.

The little black-clad women sitting at the table looked to Dusty.

Dusty stood up.

And vanished into the blue air.

33

THE RAIN CLICKED on the windowpane. Dusty watched the drops gather and slide down the glass. The clouds beyond were purple, the color of storms. She thought that she was seeing and hearing the raindrops with an abnormal acuity of sound and sight. The doctor re-examined her foot, and he spoke to her while he did:

"The reason that the question *What is life?* is difficult to answer," he said, "is that we don't yet know *why* life is."

He was not looking at her as he spoke but scrutinizing her injured foot with considerable attention, his thick octagonal glasses filled mirror-like with the lavender light from the outside. He had a headlamp strapped around his skull.

"And so," he continued, "what we're really asking is why, in physical terms, why a specific material *becomes* an organism, and not something else. To answer that, we need to first understand how life has arisen from inanimate matter."

The doctor stood up and looked at her.

"Do you see?" he said.

His light was so bright that for a moment all Dusty saw

was the glowing penumbra of his form. She squinted. He extinguished the headlamp.

"I have good news," the doctor said. "You're going to live. Life rages inside you like fire, Dusty May, and your body is killing all the nasty organisms that have infiltrated you and threaten the integrity of your body. Your injury is healing."

She watched a system of multicolored planets created by his extinguished light in collaboration with her retina — watched them orbit through the blackness of her brain and then soundlessly explode.

The rain clicked on the window.

"My father knows," she said.

"Knows what?"

"How life has arisen."

"Oh?" the doctor said. "Is your father a scientist?"

She nodded.

"Are raindrops alive?"

"No."

"How about fire?"

She shook her head.

"No," the doctor said, "you're quite correct: fire does not live, and neither does rain. Your father must be a very clever man."

"He's the cleverest," she said.

"The living cell isn't a mass of matter composed of a congregation of like molecules, but a highly differentialed system: the cell is a system of co-existing phases of different constitutions. Living things are autopoietic systems, and they're also autocatalytic — meaning: they self-create, self-produce, self-maintain, and their nucleic acids replicate within the context of whole cells and work with other developmental resources during the life-cycle and are also capable of evolving by variation. Life is a pattern of chemical processes — a pattern with specific and very special properties. Life begets a similar pattern, as raindrops or the flame of a fire also do, but life *regulates* itself as fire does not, as a raindrop does not. For humans, though, Dusty May, unique among the animals for our faculty of free-will — which is to say, the rational faculty, the faculty of thought and choice — life is not *just* physical and biological, although it is certainly that: it's also psychological and epistemological. As I'm sure your father would agree. Let's ask him."

"*What?*"

The doctor smiled kindly and went to the door of his examining room. His green eyes swam like living organisms behind his thick glasses.

"Come on, Dusty May," he said. "Your father is waiting right outside the door for you."

Before Dusty had a moment to react, the doctor had flung open the door.

The big man rose up from the chair.

34

SHE SAW IMMEDIATELY that it was not her foster father at all but the man she'd observed while waiting for Jason that night in the park, and then again, not long ago, outside the coffeeshop: the man with moon-colored hair and dangling forelock and skin approximately the same hue as hers.

Dusty caught her breath.

"That's not him," she whispered.

She leapt off the examination table and ran to the doctor. She held onto his arm — almost, it seemed, hiding behind him.

The doctor, however, looked oddly unconcerned.

Even as the big man produced from somewhere inside his jacket a bat-black, bible-black SIG sauer nine millimeter handgun and leveled it at the doctor's forehead, still the doctor looked oddly unconcerned.

The big man squeezed the trigger.

There was a bluish ghost of gun-smoke and then an explosion resounding outrageously in the enclosed silence of the examination room.

The doctor crumpled at her feet.

No falter, no misstep — just one moment standing and the next as boneless-looking as a ragdoll heaped-up at her feet: the life-force gone out of him, a living thing no more.

Dusty could hear with abnormal clarity the clicking of the rain upon the windowpane. Her foot throbbed.

She was too stunned to even scream. She stared at the lifeless doctor and the lake of blood spreading over her bare feet and across the floor. This was more blood than she'd ever seen before. She couldn't believe a human body could contain so much.

"I'm sorry," the big man said to her. "It was necessary."

Dusty May stood barefoot in the blood and looked up at him. She was so horrified that she'd entirely lost her ability to speak. At that moment, a black tomcat with a white star on its face appeared from somewhere down the hallway, white-ringed tail as straight as a rod. The tomcat stood next to the big man and looked at Dusty. He tilted his head, like a dog. Then this cat stretched his right foreleg and hind left and yawned so that she saw a mouthful of small razorous teeth and a tiny tongue as pink as candy. The blood she stood among was covering her feet. Dusty felt little things move everywhere inside her, surging. And then she felt something else, a glimpse of something — something important — but she couldn't pinpoint precisely what it was: a distant memory, perhaps, or an insight which she must revisit.

At last, she felt herself able to speak.

"Did you kill Jason?" she said. "Is that how you got my money and my passport?"

The big man didn't answer.

"Will you kill me?" she said.

Still he didn't answer. He stared at her in a way that was neither kind nor menacing.

"Your father killed Jason," he said finally, "because Jason robbed you."

The lake of blood, meanwhile, had spread out into the hallway, slopping gently over the paws of the tomcat, who looked down from these incarnadine shores as if surprised, and then began lapping at the rising blood with his candy-pink tongue. Apostrophes and hyphens of blood flecked the white star on his face.

At which point, Dusty May saw in full what a moment ago she'd only glimpsed: she was dreaming and none of this was real.

And just as in her dream she realized this, the tomcat and the dead doctor and the big man before her and all the blood she stood among — it dematerialized before her eyes and dissolved into the grainy mists of her psyche, and she awoke.

35

AWOKE TO A VIOLET DAWN, and an empty space at her core in which a cold wind swirled and which seemed to her now might never be filled. She found herself for the second time alone in the examination room of the doctor's office. Raindrops clicked upon the windowpane and ran like living things down the glass. The sun was a thin raspberry stain bleeding through the clouds in the east. A mild tinnitus whistled in her ears.

She rose and went out into the hallway.

Here, under the lurid lights of the walk-in clinic, the first thing to confront her was the big man whom she'd just dreamt of and whom she'd last seen, not long ago, outside the coffeeshop. He was sitting in a chair halfway down the hallway. He stood up to meet her.

"No," she whispered.

"Dusty May," he said, "my name is Hogan Phillips." He advanced toward her one pace and extended his hand. "I assure you, I am a friend."

Dusty stepped back.

"I mean you no harm, I promise you this," he said.

At that moment, a door opened directly beside her and the doctor appeared. She leapt behind him. Her foot faintly throbbed.

"Is everything okay?" the doctor said. "This gentleman has been waiting for you for some time."

Dusty's eyes were huge and dark, infinitely dark, like the eyes of a hunted doe.

"There's someone with me who's been looking for you, Dusty May," Hogan Phillips said. "He's been very worried about you."

Just then, a young man with thin muscular arms appeared catlike from around the corner of the hallway. He was dressed in faded blue jeans. His eyes were like blots of melting chocolate. He smiled. His teeth were slightly snaggled.

"Do you recognize me?" he said to Dusty May, who almost dissolved.

She didn't speak for a long time. She stared as if wonderstruck.

"I'd recognize that scar anywhere," she said at last.

PART V

36

THE STRUCTURES STOOD between two mountain ranges, on the edge of a tumulous plain — a wild and insular area, some ninety miles west of the Lake Pyramid Paiute Reservation. In 1916, this land had been purchased by a schismatic sect of Cistercian monks, who'd sought to replicate the monastic life as practiced by Saint Benedict, and who had built here a small medieval monastery. Within four decades, however, these monks had all died out, and the monastery stood abandoned in the wide alpine gap. Thus it remained for almost fifty years: seven small structures adrift among the oceanic grass.

For brief periods of time, hunters and backpackers used the rooms as lodgings — sleeping, like the Cistercians, on the hard straw beds — but for many years the area remained only transiently inhabited. A certain air of desolate grandeur pervaded it. The ghosts of mutilated monks wandered the windy woods.

High above, the mountain basin loomed lush and remote. It was laced with a number of spring-fed tributaries. At the western edge of the basin, a much larger river fell off the cliffs and exploded into a great crucible of vapor and bubbles below. From here, the river pounded on. It pounded down through the jumbled mountain timber and then leveled out under a shaggy bluff just behind the erstwhile monastery.

Then, in June of 1992, the land was purchased by a woman of obscure provenance, about whom very little was known, except that she was not only an acrobat, but a dancer and an architect as well. She'd made a good deal of money in her buildings and in real estate. It therefore took her hardly any time at all before she'd harnessed a piece of the river for a deep swimming pool. She also had built here a lovely rolling highway that led in from the east, and finally, after demolishing the monastery, which was already sunk partway into the earth, she constructed a school — a school of motion, as she called it. This school flourished and grew, its buildings a civilizing force: strange wonders of ovoid design.

37

DAVID LED Dusty down labyrinthian corridors and dizzying passageways which were lit along each side with strips of melon-colored light. They walked side-by-side, and they walked neither rapidly nor slowly. They did not speak — except once, after they'd gotten out of his car, he told her that this is where he'd matriculated. Their footsteps made no sound on the strange surface beneath them. This place seemed to her palatial, hyper-modern, unexplored. It occurred to her then that they'd been walking for a long time.

At last the passageway opened into a doorless room with a glowing floor of dark wood and high concave ceilings. The walls of this room were composed of glass slabs, and the room was exclusively lit now with white light from outside. Beyond the farthest window lay stretched a lush wood, in whose southernmost corner a kidney-shaped quarry-lake lanced the eye with an optically devastating dazzle of water. To the right of the lake, there arose a creamy and spherical structure, which rode the sky behind it like clouds: a masterpiece of design, similar yet distinct from the building they were now in: a natural-looking outgrowth of the round quarry rocks among which it stood.

"Are you the scientist's daughter?" a sourceless voice said to Dusty.

Dusty turned.

A woman appeared.

It was a woman whose presence would not easily be forgotten. Before anything else, Dusty realized this.

The woman was not young, yet her age was impossible to gauge. She was modern. Her hair was sorrel-red and yanked back into a long ponytail, which completely revealed her strange unforgettable face. A quiet and quietly moving person, she maneuvered through space like a dancer. She had a new sort of beauty, Dusty thought. Something almost science-fictional about her, in the planes of her face and her long sharp nose and the shadows her cheekbones cast. She wore no makeup. She walked in a manner entirely unaffected. Her body, not overly thin, was in every aspect exquisite. Her eyes were large and burned inside her skull with a deep and mysterious darkness, which when she came near to Dusty seemed to be posing a riddle. Her complexion was pale in a way that made Dusty think of thick cream and buttermilk. She had an infinitely complicated mouth, with curled lips, like a creature half asleep, lips which when she spoke drew back from her small alabaster teeth, and then words wandered out like white petals in the wind. Her head swayed gracefully upon the long stalk of her neck, and her eclectic features fused and integrated — integrated as if by something from within — and at once became a face and form fascinating and lovely.

She stopped and stood in front of Dusty. She wore thin black leggings and black tank-top and light-pink ballet slippers. Her spear-shaped fingernails looked dipped in fresh blood.

"Hello, David," she said. She smiled at him without parting her lips.

"Hello-hello!"

The woman turned to Dusty.

"Sheila," David said, "I'd like you to meet my good friend Dusty May. Dusty May, I'd like you to meet my good friend Sheila O'Shaugnessy."

"It's a pleasure to meet you, Dusty May."

"It's a pleasure to meet you, Sheila O'Shaugnessy."

"Dusty and I have written each other letters over the years," David said to Sheila. He turned back to Dusty. "Sheila owns this school for acrobats, misfits, alienates, disaffiliates, recalcitrants, and other performers."

"The scientist is my foster father," Dusty said.

The woman looked at her carefully. "You want to learn the art of dance and ballet."

"Yes."

"Tell me, Dusty: Do you know what the dance is?"

Dusty shook her head.

"The dance is the mute mistress of music," the woman said. "And music always leads."

38

THE WOMAN TURNED to David and asked him if he would please do her a favor so that she might illustrate something, and he said of course. She asked him to retrieve the umbrella that hung from the back of her chair, behind her desk, and David nodded once and walked across the long room. Sheila told Dusty to closely watch him come and go.

Dusty did.

When, sixty seconds later, he returned, Sheila looked back to Dusty and spoke.

"We all move in a unique way, Dusty May," she said. She then asked Dusty if she'd carefully observed David in his movements — his posture and steps, how he held his arms and hands while he walked, and so on.

"Yes," Dusty said.

"That is the root of dance," Sheila said.

The woman then lifted her left foot, and standing upon one leg, she asked David to place the tip of the umbrella on the toe of her left slipper. He did. Sheila was now balancing the umbrella on her toe even as she balanced on one foot, and with an effortless proprioception she continued speaking.

She told Dusty that our gait and our walk, the way we move when we work or relax, the way we reach for things, our posture and our gestures and our facial expressions, our physical *motions,* she said, whether listless or lethargic or apathetic, affected or mannered or self-conscious, poised, confident, energetic, precise, loose or sloppy — they all originate from within.

She told Dusty that our movements are the physical manifestation of what is inside, and that's why each individual moves in a unique way — because, she said, humans are almost infinitely varied, and our movements disclose with mathematical precision the thoughts and emotions that shape us.

"Dance is movement made into a system," she said. "It is organized movement. Dance systematizes movement into both a science and an art. It's the physical counterpart to the music, which always comes first. In dance, you must never lose sight of the musicality. Ever. Music is the flesh made spirit. Dance is the spirit made flesh. And we are all flesh-and-blood creatures of a self-styled spirit."

Still balancing, then, with a light deft flick of her left foot, she launched the umbrella directly at Dusty May.

It came through the air quickly.

Dusty lifted her hand and caught it without apparent effort or surprise.

Sheila smiled.

39

THE NEXT DAY broke breathless and raggedy for Dusty May, who on that breathless and raggedy day was initiated into the mysteries and intricacies of the dance and ballet.

This was the day Dusty learned among other things that her straight legs and her limbs — which were long for her size — her strong back as well, her high foot-arches and her proportionate body, her understanding of her body, they were assets, Sheila said to her, her fitness and physicality giving her what Sheila called an easy turnout.

Sheila also told Dusty May, and then showed her through physical demonstration, the meaning of the terms *porte-de-bras, plié, sauté, arabesque, pirouette, tendu, elevé, relevé, coupés,* and *fouettés* — but more valuable still:

It was on this wild breathless afternoon that Dusty was initiated into secrets of the body human in all its elegant complexity: kinesiology, biology, musicology and the human ear, the black art of anatomy — which things soon became for Dusty the foundation of a kinetic awareness and depth of understanding that would shape her own body and being into something at once powerful, fast, nimble, poised.

It would also impart upon her a grace and sense of presence and space and an esthetic elongation for purposes of her carriage and her line, as well as a depth of understanding which Dusty quickly came to crave. She came to crave this learning for its own sake, for the enrichment she felt it bestowing upon her solitary life, which was so internal and lonesome and pure.

Every loneliness is rarified, Sheila said to her, a rarified summit, especially when it's for the sake of self-development.

This also marked for Dusty May the beginning of grueling eight-hour-a-day practice sessions, then ten-hour, then twelve — every day — not because she was forced to but because she wanted it.

Yet more than anything, this was when Sheila O'Shaugnessy first taught Dusty to listen to music in a more cerebral and fundamental way — after which, music for Dusty May was transmuted into a kind of immanent force that spread throughout her body, rooting itself so deeply inside her that she felt no one and no thing could ever touch it, like the glowing force at the core of her being, which was her essence, and with which music soon became interchangeable, synonymous: a music inside her impervious to virulent organisms and outside forces. Thereafter, Dusty would often be seen listening to music as if searching for something hidden inside the melodies, eyes closed, sitting or standing, her hands and arms moving almost unconsciously, in ghost-like *porte-de-bras*.

The white feet of Sheila beat winglike across the dark-wooden floors, a sound of fluttering wings, her feather-light body whirling like wind across dark water, as she simultaneously spoke, saying that creativity and greatness are more possible to humans than most humans realize, and that the

biggest obstacle to these things is the strength and willing-
ness to do the work required, because the effort is large, and
it always will be large, she said, because every exalted and
rarified thing is difficult, and that is why mediocrity is
commonplace.

"Scientifically," Sheila said, "the basis of life — the
energy of life, as Aristotle called it, an innate impulse to
animation and activity — is simply the desire for expression. Creative expression is a natural extension of one's
exuberance for life, and vice acts as a counter-agent to that
exuberance — the word *vice* itself coming from the Latin
word *vitium,* which means 'fault' or 'frailty,' a breach in the
integrity of a thing, not in reference to humans exclusively
but to structures and other things as well, both living and
non-living. In humans, *vitium* is that which smothers life
and prevents the living thing from having life most
abundantly."

Dusty watched her with those infinitely black eyes that
did not miss anything.

Eyes which told nothing of what was going on inside her
moving mind.

40

"IF YOU BRING FORTH that which is within you, it will uplift you," Sheila said. "If you don't bring forth what is within you, what you do not bring forth will destroy you."

"What is that?" Dusty said.

"It is a half quote."

"What does it mean?

"It means that fulfilling the promise which your brain and body contain will give you more abundant life, while ignoring your promise has the power to destroy you. It means that doing the things which cultivate your living potential are good. The things that stunt it are bad."

Dusty didn't reply.

"Tell me," Sheila said. "Do you know the precise meaning of the words *integrate* and *integral* and *integer* and *integrity?*"

Dusty thought for a moment and then shook her head. "Not well enough to put into words," she said.

"They mean entire, whole, all of a piece. They mean the same on the outside as on the inside."

Dusty was silent.

"When we speak of a bridge or some other structure as having integrity," Sheila said, "we mean that the structure is whole. It is entire. When the integrity of a structure has been breached, the structure is in danger. Do you remember one of the first things you said to me when we were alone in this room? You said that you'd never seen a building like this. Would you like to know why?"

"Yes."

"Because most people build things as they build their lives: randomly, whimsically, chaotically, without focus or purpose or a theme to unify them. When something is unified by a single theme, as this building is, it is integrated. It is whole. Constructing a building or a life upon fleeting, ephemeral, transient premises or values renders that life or building perpetually unstable and shaky. Truly integrated things are unshakable, unbreakable."

Once again, Dusty remained mute, but a slight crease appeared above the bridge of her nose. The strange lovely woman watched her and even resisted an impulse to reach over and, with her thumb, softly smooth out Dusty's dark forehead-crease, the older woman's ivorine flesh so pale next to Dusty's swarthy skin.

"The body and the brain also require a unifying theme," Sheila said. "Yes," she continued, "that's right. If they don't have an integrated theme, they're at war. Now, then. Think of music as brain. Think of dance as body. Music and dance together represent the integration of body and brain. But it's you who must integrate them."

41

FOR ONE YEAR STRAIGHT, Dusty practiced every single day — eight, ten, twelve hour days, though recrudescing injuries and ominous tremors appeared and reappeared almost from the beginning.

The first tremor came when a mysterious barrister showed up at the door of the circus-school and made odd inquiries concerning the curriculum and practice regimen. This man was small and strange-looking, late-fifties, perhaps, somehow buffoonish, and yet with a certain sapience that glinted like butcher knives in his hazel eyes. His hair was dark and wispy, his skull lobe-shaped and large in proportion to the rest of his body, a reedy neck and prominent Adam's apple and spindly arms. That morning, he'd not shaved carefully, and three missed whiskers stood thorn-like along his throat. He asked probing questions which Sheila did not answer either affirmatively or negatively — "purely perfunctory," the man said, "governmental record-keeping" — and with his hands clasped behind his back, he left the premises bowing and making deferential nods and mows and apologies like a lost and wandered simpleton, which, however, he was not.

He left also a small envelope that contained his card: Hollis D. Nickles, Esquire.

Ten days after that, Dusty's toenails cracked from her long hours spent in deliberate practice: thin fissures that ran like spiderlegs down the toenails of both feet. Still, she did not relent or scale back the rigorousness or the amount of her practice hours.

Then, in learning the importance of feet and ballet and in learning to point her feet beautifully, her toes next began to bleed — intermittently, at first, and then continually, so that within three months, she bled daily through her socks. She taped her toes and anointed them with salve and took B-vitamins, which helped, but it didn't completely cure her: her feet now were always bleeding and sore, and there were also still occasional flashes of pain that shot from her old heel injury to her ankle and into her slender calf, and she thought she saw her toes already growing malformed, as if little creatures inside her had warped her limbs and digits to a will of their own.

Shortly after which, she found something at the very bottom of the swimming pool that unnerved her beyond all normal proportion.

42

IT WAS JUST A HAIRLINE CRACK, she thought, like a tiny lightning bolt running along the bottom of the deep green pool. It was barely noticeable and hardly serious. Why, then, this sense of dread?

She wasn't sure. Yet she couldn't stop thinking about it.

The pool was huge and circular and deep — not an olympic pool of clear and shimmering turquoise but emerald-green and dark, with something loch-like about it: vast and cold, a training ground for daredevil divers and esoteric aquatic performers.

Virtually every morning, when the pool was completely unoccupied and silent, Dusty swam here.

She breast-stroked laps. She was fast and fluid. But she also enjoyed swimming underwater and, like a pearl-diver, holding her breath as long as she possibly could — longer and longer every day, so that, after a few weeks, she was able to maintain one breath for over three minutes, kicking and paddling deep down in these cold and prasine keeps.

This was how she'd noticed the crack in the integrity of the floor.

Three days after first discovering it, when she'd just finished lap-swimming and was hanging onto the cement side, the lapping waves sloshing over her arm and into the slurping gutter drain, she heard the door open and then saw through chlorine-bleared eyes and her goggles a man stride through and into the pool-room. He was barefoot and shirtless. She didn't recognize him, but she could see in his movements and manner that he was strong and formidable.

He stood for a moment on the far side of the circular pool, some two-hundred feet away from Dusty. His hair was honey-blonde. He scanned the emerald waters. Dusty watched him. She didn't move. He appeared not to notice her. After sixty seconds, he pivoted on his foot and left. The crash of the closing door behind him resounded clangorously in the acoustical pool-room.

Dusty blinked slowly behind her beaded goggles. At length, still hanging onto the side of the pool, she removed her swim-cap which felt like a tightening band of iron around her skull. She rested three minutes more. Then she took several deep breaths, holding in the last and the largest, and submerged herself.

She swam down into the clean cold water.

With rising apprehension, she flipper-kicked to the spot where she thought the crack was located.

She found it quickly.

She stopped swimming and let her body go slack. The pool was illuminated with mint-green lights embedded here and there along the bottom of the cement floor.

Cautiously, she reached out her hand and ran her finger along the crack. It felt to her like a cut or a bone-fracture in the body of this beautiful building which now housed her. Her heart pounded. She traced the fracture lightly with her first finger and then her first two fingers, moving from bottom-to-top, top-to-bottom.

What was it she felt in caressing this slick wet wound? Sorrow? Sorrow mixed with fear?

Just then, she thought she caught movement on the upper margin of her vision, and when she looked up, she indeed saw a sea-pale figure swimming directly toward her.

Her heart leapt.

The figure arrived with astonishing speed.

It was the man she'd seen moments before standing on the edge of the pool surveying the waters.

He swam like a gentle cetacean, his whole body undulant and muscular. And yet there was something in the way he knifed through the water that had about it the appetite of an elasmobranch fish. He wore a white swim cap but no mask or goggles or breathing apparatus, and he at first appeared to her bald-headed. When he got to within five feet of her, he smiled and raised his eyebrows, so that his forehead pleated, like a whale's brow.

Dusty did not swim away. Something held her. She continued to hang there in the jade-green depths, two feet from the bottom. She was now starting to notice her need for oxygen. She watched him. The man, still smiling, gave her a thumbs-up — and then, in the same motion, he did something which for some reason made her wince:

He took this same thumb and arced it down through the water and ran his thumb along the fissure, just as she'd run her fingers along it.

She thought she felt it, as if the wound were her own.

He ran his thumb over the fracture and simultaneously looked at her. In that moment, an indescribable transference passed between them, a tacit and mutual understanding of great depth and seriousness — at which point

Dusty resolved that no matter how short her oxygen supply, she would not leave here before him.

She saw furthermore the same resolution gather in his unoccluded eyes — even as a chain of silver bubbles issued from his mouth when he smiled at her again — even as her windpipe contracted within her neck and her Indian-black hair floated like seaweed in the green water, and she hung there as motionless as a suicide.

43

A FULL MINUTE PASSED.

Wild and starved for oxygen, she felt herself going inwardly berserk. She forced herself to remain as inert as possible, barely fluttering above the elephant-gray floor, which at some point — she did not know when — she'd come to think of as a living thing with a heartbreaking wound.

She blinked slower and slower.

His pale body meanwhile drifted five feet across from her. The mint-colored light looked unreal and ghostly upon his skin. He stared at her through the unreal light, in this watery world which for both of them had now become everything. Soon his smile vanished. He thrashed a little, like a hooked fish.

Her lungs jerked involuntarily behind her breastbone — jerked over and over, revolting at her mind's willful deprivation of air. Every part of her body called for her to come exploding up into the oxygenated world, to breathe, breathe. Yet she did not. So that suddenly now in these cold emerald chambers, she thought she might very well die of willful suffocation.

Another fifteen seconds passed.

All was silent.

He paddled harder, more frantically. She did not seem to notice him.

Ten more seconds passed.

She felt crazed now with underwater panic and on the brink of unconsciousness. Still, she didn't thrash or move at all. She forced herself to remain inanimate. The subsurface currents licked her heavy hair.

She fixed her eyes on the crack below her. She was dimly aware that she was no longer in her right mind. All at once, she felt her eyes slam shut and a kind of calm wave roll through her body.

She did not know how much more time elapsed, but when she opened her eyes again, she saw that the sea-pale man had gone, a silver chain of bubbles in his wake.

She was all alone at the bottom of the pool, floating in the ghostly light. She had outlasted him, but at what cost? And just as she thought her brain would go dark, she pushed herself with both feet and all her remaining strength off the cement floor.

She imagined she felt the spider-leg fracture beneath her toes.

She came rocketing up to the surface.

In her delirious state, rising through the green water for what seemed minutes, her mind played tricks — and the moment she began to think she might not make it after all, she broke the surface and sucked in the air as she'd never sucked it in before.

She rolled over onto her back and gasped. Her huge heart hammered in the chambers of her chest.

She stared at the high vaulted ceiling overhead, like a breathing bell. The next thing she knew, a warm dry hand was gently helping her out of the water.

It was David.

44

It was David as well whom she now told calmly in her half-crazed state that he mattered more to her than anyone, because he'd always been good to her and kind — she could *feel* his kindness, she said, always, and goodness is timeless, violation death — and it was also David to whom she revealed her fear that Kenneth Dvorak had, in her wildest conjectures, infiltrated this school of systematized motion and acrobatic art: infiltrated it, she said, with organisms in a kind of germ warfare, so that the integrity of the entire school was now in jeopardy, as if its architecture were being dismantled from deep within. She told David that she was afraid he would destroy everything because of her, and that she would never be free of Kenneth Dvorak.

David cocked his head and cast her a long steady stare. He did not say anything. An idea he'd already been considering now came back into his mind, but from a different angle, and with renewed force.

He dropped his eyes to the green water and squinted at the spanking waves.

Later that same night, he phoned his mother, whose

name was Bird, and who was still in shock over the loss of her husband Wesson Weekly — not grieving him in any conventional sense, not regretting his loss, but half resenting him. Why hadn't he told her? And what could this orphan girl have meant to him that he should go to such unthinkable extremes?

"Hello, David," she said.

"I have an important question I must ask."

"Yes?"

"Is Kenneth Dvorak my real father?"

Bird was silent for a long time. "Why do you ask that?" she said.

"Is he?"

"Yes," she said. "He is."

Finally, it was David again who, one month later, while practicing a handstand high atop a bongo balance-board stacked atop another bongo balance-board, lowered himself into a planche push-up position and then, with astonishing grace and balance and full-body strength, swung his legs slowly around, as he had countless times before, so that his entire torso and lower-half were twisted elegantly horizontal and perfectly perpendicular the direction he was facing, and then lifting one hand, holding this one-armed planche with his lower body still so elegantly contorted and plank-like, suddenly felt the integrity of his wrist give way — and without any warning whatsoever, the balance-board cracked as well. For the first time in his circus life, he fell from a great height.

Dusty alone, watching him practice as she so often did from the dark distance of theater seats, leapt horrified to her bleeding feet.

45

He was not injured seriously — a hairline fracture in his left wrist and a mild concussion from the fall — but in the hospital, he developed a lung infection, which then turned into pleurisy. The doctors therefore kept him. They swathed his whole midsection in a thin and foam-like pre-wrap and then tightly wound athletic tape around this.

"Presumably to keep me from coughing myself to pieces," David told Dusty, who had come to visit him.

He smiled softly. His large wet cow eyes gleamed in the half-light.

"Are you okay?" she said.

"Yes."

For perhaps the ten-thousandth time in the last few weeks, she looked at the long scar that ran seam-like down the length of his face to his jugular. It had turned white over the years. She did not know why the sight of this scar touched her so, why it always had. She resisted an impulse to reach out and gently trace it with her first two fingers.

"But if I'm going to be here much longer, I wish I could

see the stars and the moon outside my window," he said. "I have trouble sleeping, and it calms me to look at them."

"Why can't you? See the stars and the moon, I mean."

"The streetlights are right there, and they blot out the night."

Dusty went to the drapeless window. His room was two floors up. The hospital quad lay spread out below. It was illuminated by a phalanx of streetlamps, two of which stood directly outside the glass, five feet away. They gave off a light that was sterile and white.

She appeared at once very thoughtful. "I have always loved the stars too fondly to be fearful of the night," she said to the glass.

"Is that yours?" he said.

"No. It's from an English poet and novel-writer named Sarah Williams — often misattributed to Galileo." She hesitated. "According to Kenneth," she said.

David watched her with pensive eyes from his hospital bed. Piano music came through his radio.

"How much longer will they keep you?" she said. She was still looking philosophically out the window. Below, a carload of young people in a red convertible cruised past: whooping and shrieking and laughing and drinking on this, their day off, and she thought, not judgmentally but as a matter of pure observation, there was something fundamentally different in the way people experienced relaxation compared with her. She thought she should pursue this insight, that it was in some way very significant, but the music from the radio suddenly soared, and she shut her eyes, her mind pulled inexorably away.

"Another week," David said. "They're worried about pneumonia. And staph."

She felt something hammer deep down inside her body,

and her old heel injury pulsed. She took in the music. At last she opened her eyes.

She turned back to David. She stared at his dark muscular fingers splayed like a starfish on the white cotton sheets.

He smiled at her again.

Her lips broke open in return, disclosing the thin blue cleft between her two front teeth.

Five minutes later, on her way from the hospital, her black sneakers squeaking down the shiny tiles, she approached the doctor on duty. This woman had short chestnut hair and a nervous facial tick, and she gazed vacantly at Dusty when Dusty asked if the streetlights outside room 222 could be shut off.

"No," the doctor said, "absolutely not. Why do you ask?"

Dusty was about to explain — explain about the stars and the moon — but then she thought better of it.

"Thank you," Dusty said.

Yet that very night, just as darkness fell, the white lights outside room 222, and a few others besides, were suddenly abolished, so that the moon and the stars shone brightly through the window of his room.

46

THE NEXT MORNING, hospital maintenance was called in to repair the lights. These men found nothing wrong with the bulbs but discovered instead a tripped circuit-breaker behind a box outside the cafeteria, which was in the rear of the hospital. This would have gone unnoticed, except in this case the lock on the circuit-breaker box had been picked. Still, maintenance didn't think too much of it: one man reset the switch, and the sterile white lights bloomed back on.

That same night, however, these very lights went out again, and the following evening, after resetting the switch for the second time, two men stationed themselves in the cab of a pick-up truck in the parking lot outside the cafeteria.

Just as darkness fell, they saw a small thin figure in a mushroom-shaped cap move swiftly in, pick the lock of the breaker box, and trip the breakers. The figure came and went so fast that the two men scarcely had time to act.

The same thing happened the next night, but this time, the men were ready.

The small figure swept in with the darkness and tripped

the breakers and turned to leave — and the men leapt from the truck. One called out:

"Stop!"

The figure did not stop but ran.

The men gave chase. They barreled through the darkness. They chased after the figure, who astounded them with such lightness, such a nimble quick manner of moving — electric with life and the life-force that this body contained, like a little Spring-Heeled Jack resurrected in twenty-first century America, in black tennis shoes and a mushroom-shaped cap and a maize-yellow shirt they could not see which said RUN WILD, now ducking beneath a row of parked cars and then vanishing, moonlight and starlight trailing behind her like pixie dust.

PART VI

47

IN THE ROOM of toys and dolls, a ponderous panda sat with open arms on the polished wooden floor and stared life-lessly at Dusty with big button eyes the same color as her own. He had a pink tongue poking out a smiling mouth and was flanked on either side by freckle-faced ventriloquist dolls with carmine lips. A life-sized zebra flashed behind. A row of large green wine bottles stood under the windows, and a living cat of butterscotch-and-black lay couchant on the floor beneath. The room glowed like a jewel. Beautiful piano music seeped into the room from unseen speakers.

Dusty watched as Sheila with a supple wrist animated an ostrich-marionette made of styrofoam and wires but plumed with real feathers. Dusty watched as Sheila brought the bird to life and marched it right up to Dusty and then made the ostrich rub its feathered forehead across Dusty's fingers.

"I brought you here to illustrate for you again the essential principle of life," Sheila said, "to tell you again that the energy of life is the impulse to motion and activity, which in living things is self-generated and which in humans begins in the brain. What is the mind if not motion in the mental realm?"

Dusty did not answer. She narrowed her eyes on the brainless marionette of wires and styrofoam.

"The essence of thought, as the essence of life, is growth," Sheila said. "And the opposite of growth is still-ness. Death is inertia. Creative expression is a natural exten-sion of one's enthusiasm for movement and life. And ballet is movement made into an art and a science."

Who was this splendid woman, Dusty thought, with such deep green eyes and vivid vital presence — such an abounding interest and with an aura of self-contained isola-tion, who sought to uplift her?

Sheila told Dusty that people can easily hide or keep private who they really are or facets of who they really are and that this is not necessarily a bad thing, but that in both the act of creative expression and also the response to creative expression, the total personality is exactly revealed and cannot be hidden.

Sheila said furthermore that the choice of subject-matter in both the creator and also the viewer, whether the subject-matter be joyful, degenerate, redemptive, cruel, boring, beautiful, debased, immature, inspirational, macabre, silly, smart, or anything else or any combination, it unswervingly reveals what things both the creator and also the person who responds to this artwork regard as signifi-cant in life and in the universe — while the style, Sheila said, whether clear, convoluted, crisp, unfocused, clean, confusing, elegant, sloppy, sophisticated, vulgar, noetic, poetic, or any cross-combination, reveals precisely the way both the creator and also the viewer *think*. She said this was as true for pictures and paintings and posters as it was for music and movies and books and sculpture and dance.

"Style reveals the mind in motion," Sheila said. "It shows how the mind moves and how the consciousness operates. Style is How. Subject is What. Style is technique, and technique is personality. What does that personality regard as important, and how does that personality express it? Subject and style are united by a theme. Theme is meaning."

At that moment, the little living black-and-butterscotch cat rose and stretched, hind-leg and foreleg simultaneously, and then leapt up to the windowsill and from here stepped down onto the row of wine bottles and walked lightly across them. The bottles did not move.

Dusty watched.

Sheila watched her watch.

The cat walked across all the bottles and then slid like water back onto the floor and rested.

"What will your theme be, Dusty May?"

Dusty looked from the cat to Sheila.

"Can I just choose?" Dusty said. "Just like that, I mean?" And softly, softly Dusty snapped her fingers next to her own ear.

"Yes," Sheila said.

Dusty didn't reply. Her eyes went back to the couchant cat.

"Passion is willed," Sheila said. "It's not inborn. Talent is learned. Talent, like passion, is developed. The word *passion* comes from the Latin word *pati,* which means 'to suffer.' Talent requires dedication, which, as you of all people know, is difficult. But no matter the endeavor, the process is identical: you decide and then you act. You learn and then you do. Do you know the fundamental mistake most people make?"

"No."

"They don't choose their theme. A central purpose *is* a unifying theme."

"What do they do instead?"

"They let outside forces choose it for them."

"How?"

"By not thinking for themselves, by uncritically accepting what they've been brought up among, by following whatever stimulus happens to attract them or give them immediate gratification, until those things progress into vice. Their theme is in this way determined by something other than their own fundamental will."

Dusty was silent. The sunlight poured into the room, igniting the agate eyes of the stuffed zebra, so that those two eyes flickered purple and blue.

"He once brought me back to life," Dusty said. She was staring not at Sheila but at the sunlight burning life-like in the zebra's eyes.

"Who?" Sheila said.

"Kenneth Dvorak, my foster father."

"What happened?"

"I was twelve. I was wading across the river, and the current was too strong. It swept me under — under a tangle of sticks — and I drowned. He dove in and pulled me out, but my heart had stopped."

Only now did Dusty look from the sunlight back to Sheila.

"I was dead," Dusty said, "and he revivified me. He breathed life back into me. A part of me will always love him more than I love anyone — not because of this alone but because he gave me so much life in so many different ways, and he taught me so many things, and he loved me properly in return. I *felt* the genuineness of his love for me, and it meant the world to me."

Sheila was silent. She regarded Dusty for a long time. The sunlight fell around them like pollen. The piano music pulsed rhythmically. Sheila reached over and turned up the volume, and then she put her hand out, and Dusty gripped Sheila's hand in her own.

"The dance is life," Sheila said. "Death, violation: where is thy sting?"

Then Sheila danced Dusty across the gorgeous glowing floor of wood, through this sunlit space, where the zebra and the panda and the dummies stared mutely from their situated place, and the living kitten watched so alert and curious with those jeweled eyes in that mottled face.

48

A CHOCOLATE-BROWN SPIDER sat with pie-eyes in the center
of her web, a silken egg-sac slung beneath her. The web
hung like a miniature trampoline under the eaves of the
house, the strands of gossamer flickering lilac-to-lavender in
the soft breeze and the fading sunlight, a twig snagged like a
chicken bone in the web. The evening sky grew coral. Far
away to the north, sultry cloud-monsters were dissolving
and reforming, dissolving and reforming, constantly over
the horizon. An almost blood-like smell spiked the air, an
odor of raw meat mixed with something musty and vinous.

David stared at the spider for a long time: lady of the
loom, motionless, microcephalic, but with a body as big as a
child's fist.

"Hello, David," said a sonorous voice behind him.

Before David pivoted, he saw in the reluctent windowpane of the front door the foreshortened image of a man
rendered small in its pink reflection.

David turned.

Kenneth Dvorak stood twenty feet away, under a solitary
apple tree among swaying grass, the limbs of the tree bent

low with its lunar globes of fruit. He was dressed in a char-
coal suit and black tie, his white shirt glistering. He had an
old-fashioned pocketwatch, affixed to a silver chain, and he
consulted it now. Then he wound it up. A murder of crows
watched from the topmost limbs of the apple tree. Kenneth
Dvorak's face was calm and handsome. His stature and his
presence were very great.

He smiled. His hairless head gave back the crimson light
bleeding through the delicate fabric of the evening sky.

"Hello, father," David said.

"I thought you'd come. I hoped you would."

The smell of raw meat grew stronger.

"Os ex ossibus meis et caro de carne," Kenneth Dvorak said.
"Bone of my bone, flesh of my flesh."

David watched him. For a full minute, neither spoke. In
the field beyond, a lone poplar pulsed in the wind. The sky
darkened to burgundy. The wind went warmly about
David's hair.

"I have something to ask," David said.

Kenneth Dvorak advanced toward him. The tall grass
swished against his high boots. He came to within four feet
and stopped. He towered above his son by over twelve
inches, physically dwarfing him, but he did not dwarf the
clean immutable healthiness of David's body. The spider
twitched. Kenneth Dvorak's eyeballs — and only his
eyeballs — went briefly to the web and then back to David.
"Ask," he said.

"I want you to do this for Dusty May," David said. "I've
never asked you for anything, and this is the only thing I'll
ever ask of you."

David then stepped forward a pace and leaned closer to
the mountainous man who was his father by blood.
Speaking softly, he told Kenneth Dvorak what he wanted

him to do, and explained why, proposing a kind of wager or a final test of justice, which test would decide everything, and in which Kenneth Dvorak would organize and fund and promote a contest of human motion. If Dusty won, David said, she would be exonerated. Kenneth Dvorak listened with great interest and seriousness, the smell of blood now clangorous between them, while in the boughs above, the murder of crows watched with golden eyes, and then Kenneth Dvorak grinned and nodded and said yes, he would do this thing, and he would win.

One of the crows resituated its wing, as if that wing had been improperly folded.

A quarter mile away, at the foot of the iron mountains, thermal winds swirled up scarves of dust, and the slow deep river that ran below the mountains reflected the bloody evening sky in a perfect replica, so that the river now looked like a vat of blood, and in the spider web behind David, the translucent silk sac split noiselessly, and all the eggs hatched open, and an army of baby spiders poured out and began eating the mother.

David did not see any of this.

But Kenneth Dvorak did. The wind, the water, and the blood, he said to himself.

49

In the dream, Dusty May came alone to the room of toys and dolls. The room was darkling. A doll with X's for eyes and a gap-toothed grin hung naked from the ceiling. A brutal gash circumscribed the little porcelain neck from which fresh spurts of water and blood freely disgorged. An army of tiny bugs streamed in and out of the doll's nose and mouth and ears and eyes, infiltrating her and destroying her from within. Dusty turned her head away. A cold wind swirled into the room and slammed the door shut.

"Do you know what the space between your front teeth represents, Dusty May?"

Dusty looked across the room. The vast and naked corpus of Kenneth Dvorak stood glowing from among the shadows. She did not reply to him.

"It represents the empty space in your life that will never be filled," he said.

She turned away again. A warm and gentle thing brushed against her leg. She looked down. It was the black-and-butterscotch kitty walking slowly around her. She could hear its purr, feel the life-force burning within the soft body, and she thought of life and death and blood, and she thought of violation. She shut her eyes.

When she opened them again, Sheila was in the room. She appeared like an angel. She had a white hyacinth in her hair, and her hair was loose and flowing. Her veins ran like little azure streams all across her body — veins containing her blood which poured life into her and throughout her. She was very lovely. Sheila looked at the silent naked figure of Kenneth Dvorak, and she did not remove her eyes from him, even as she spoke to Dusty. As she spoke, the shadows of the room engulfed him more profoundly.

Sheila told Dusty that Kenneth Dvorak was wrong and that the space between her teeth, far from representing emptiness, was a testament to Dusty's irrepressible happiness and her beautiful smile, the music that throbbed inside her which no thing could infiltrate or break. She said that emotional intimacy is the very bedrock of love, never fading but obtaining, and that this warm intimacy flows naturally from the wellspring of her happiness and is more fundamental than physical appetites and evanescent pleasures no matter how voracious or ecstatic, which pleasures will always fade, and she said that love in the deepest sense stems fundamentally from the capacity to value. She said that this capacity starts and ends with the independent self and the independent mind that thinks and reasons and loves itself first for the very capacity it has to do this: a mind of indestructible balance.

Her radiant figure transmogrified before Dusty's eyes into the colossal enormity of Kenneth Dvorak, who now wore a long white lab coat and who she in that moment felt had in many ways created and shaped her.

Toys and dolls and mannequins came alive all around him, animated at his lightest touch, and in the subfusc dreamlight of Dusty's psyche, they marched through the room like trained animals and players at a psychedelic circus: illbedowered merrymakers and gnomes and elves and red-bearded trolls, the doll-like little man with perfect DNA ringlets and the vampiric women who were his ventriloquist dummies, the trotting zebra with dull-purple eyes and the laughing panda and marionettes stepping ponderously, all conjured as from a demented man's nightmare, and in the dream Dusty pleaded with Dvorak to disengage his reckless experimentation with violence and germs and living things and destruction. She told him that humans are not toys to be tinkered with — at which he smiled so broadly that his big cubic teeth glowed phosphorescent, and she could see his hot-pink uvula hanging from the cave-maw of his mouth and dripping like a stalactite onto the rough carpeting of his tongue.

He answered her that his merrymaking was merely the rearrangement of God's indestructible matter, which possesses no will of its own but acts and reacts as it must in strict adherence to the nature with which God endowed it — a kind of cosmic imperative, he said, a vital dust — and that humans alone possess the power to impose order upon God's creation, and impose it they do and properly should, like legends on a map. He said that absent conceptual consciousness, there is no order or disorder, as there is no time: the universe is timeless in the literal sense — it is out of time — and there are only entities which act through purely casual forces, neither orderly nor disorderly but in total accord with their identity, and that that species which can rearrange God's matter has become a god, insofar as this species can now rearrange the very architecture of the universe whose integrity is unimpeachable and perfect.

He told her finally that the most potent germ he'd ever

discovered was with him at this precise moment, as it was always with him, and would she like to see it?

When Dusty didn't answer yes or no, he extricated from the pocket of his long lab coat a pyrex test-tube that looked empty but was labeled and tightly corked and across which was a vertical strip of tape with letters in his own beautiful handwriting. Those letters said: IDEAS. Underneath this he'd inked a small and intricate-looking skull and crossbones.

The moment Dusty awoke she heard herself say aloud but softly in her half-sleep:

"Don't you know you were an actual father to me, and I loved you very much?"

50

Dusty kept the torn-out magazine page inside a book. It was a book her foster mother had given her long ago — a book of stories that Dusty loved: stories set in strange Patagonian lands. Dusty always carried this book safely in her backpack, and she opened it now.

She unfolded the magazine page, which she'd carefully torn from the magazine in her foster father's library not quite two years before. It was the black-and-white image of the magical human who danced catlike upon wine bottles.

Dusty showed this image now to Sheila, who then asked Dusty if she knew where themes come from.

Dusty shook her head.

"Ideas," Sheila said. "Themes come from ideas. This is why not all themes are equal."

"What do you mean?"

"I mean that just as some ideas are smart and sound and true, while other ideas are false and destructive, so it is with themes: some are life-giving and life-affirming and fulfilling. Others are themes of banality or defeat or corrosion or human ineptitude and purposelessness."

Dusty was silent. Sheila scrutinized the image Dusty had passed her.

"What does this photo and this dance represent to you?" Sheila said.

"Skill and mastery and perfect balance," Dusty said.

"Tell me why, specifically."

"Because I think dancing en pointe on wine bottles requires just that: skill and perfect balance," Dusty said. "And lightness."

Sheila smiled. "Why lightness?"

"Because cats are light and agile."

"They're also resilient and independent. They're strong, mysterious, self-contained little creatures," Sheila said, even as the piebald kitty walked into the room and advanced toward them both. "Like you."

Dusty looked to the floor, where the cat now circled her legs. Dusty reached down and stroked her head.

"What will your theme be, Dusty May?"

Dusty didn't immediately answer. She bent down and gently lifted and cradled the kitty in her arms. She could feel the vital hum, the feline purr against her chest.

"Lightness," Dusty said. "Lightness and joy."

51

"Do you still want to be a dancer?" David said to Dusty.

"Yes," Dusty said. "Very much."

"I want to tell you something," David said. "Please listen." He looked at her. "Do you remember a letter you once wrote me which, with great insight, said that you didn't believe there was really such a thing as natural talent because you knew from firsthand experience how hard and how time-consuming the practice and the work required to develop a skill?"

Dusty nodded.

"What I want to tell you is this: in sheer singlemindedness and discipline and focus, I've never seen anyone like you, or anything even close. This is why, Dusty May, no matter what happens, you'll always succeed: because your spirit is unbreakable, and it is an inspiration to us all, as you are."

He smiled and so did she, and then she began to weep.

"Come, Dusty May," he said. "It's time."

"Time?" she said, with alarm. "Time for what?"

"Time to go away and train alone with Sheila O'Shaugnessy. Time to decide your fate. Time to murder and create."

52

TOURNAMENT NIGHT in a sweltering Las Vegas stadium, and the girl with the gap-toothed smile danced bleeding in her ballet slippers. The sodium lights of the arena lay upcast on the low-hanging sky above. There was an electrical charge in the air: a crackling undercurrent that came neither from the lights nor from the distant heat lightning, but from the galvanized excitement of the crowd.

The long banner floating above her said, in huge crimson letters:

A CONTEST OF MOTION

Dusty May danced lightly across the empty bottles which stood upon the balance beam, and she moved with so much purity and grace, so sweetly, that the riveted crowd went dead silent. Like a water-spider on the surface of the stream, she skated across the bottles.

There was an indescribably subtle rhythm in her, not a sway but a rhythmic ripple, a motion coming from some music sourced so deeply inside her that not even she herself knew how far down it went. This music which was her essence poured out of her — from the top of her head to the tips of her bleeding toes — and the entire stadium heard it and felt it. They saw it. They saw it in her every movement, and they saw it in the expression stamped upon her face: the absolute focus which imbued her and which glowed with such a radiant sense of skill and competence and controlled thought in motion — the discipline of her reasoning brain.

They gazed at her in awe and stupefaction, the little catlike girl in real-life upon the stage, but her televised image broadcast and blown-up to superhuman proportions upon silver screens all throughout the stadium. Two of the cameras focused exclusively, in close-up, on her pink ballet slippers now soaked vermillion. The onlookers watched agog.

They watched agog, and they watched in suspense her dance-routine of balance and lightness pulsing in perfect time with the joyous music, which cut through the air like a blade, entering her human ears and sliding down through those channels and then into the channels of her brain that transmuted the music into movement. They saw the stupendous power her little body contained. They felt it, felt the life-force inside her which was as vast and as deep as the deep green sea.

Rising, lifting herself higher, pointing her toes beautifully, she was now electrocuted by a blast of whitehot pain that shot from her calf to the bottom of her foot and then into her cracked toes which were bleeding through her ballet slippers, and she thought: he's trying to prevent me from uplifting myself. And though her energy was boundless, her strength and the depth of her brain bottomless inside the living body which housed her human spirit — still, near the end now, it came apart in a violent physical explosion:

Sixty seconds left in her difficult antic dance, hopping lightly from the last bottle back onto the balance beam, prancing en point and then down onto full-foot stability and launching into a front-flip dismount, Dusty landed a little off on the ungiving floor. This caused her to prepare wrong for her next step: an arabesque into a series of en pointe *fouettés*.

She felt a hammer blow deep inside her body, and then there was a dull pop that sounded to the audience like a ghastly thud.

The integrity of her left ankle gave way the moment just before she went into that final series of *fouettés*.

The ankle snapped and her foot flopped the other way.

The audience gasped as one.

The people who had come to see this contest of movement had come here to be entertained. They all expected they'd leave once the excitement had risen and fallen, after which they'd go back to their half-chosen lives and their half-chosen friends, the lunches and the dinners and the drinks and all the parties and party-people and the fleeting pleasures and the endless partisan discussions and news-cycles, and the drudgery of jobs that did not fulfill: an existence of ennui, an existence of strangled hopes and stillborn dreams, the unacknowledged ache of desires left unreached for, desires left blowing like dying leaves along the edge of a beautiful but long lonesome road down which no real progress had ever been made. Yet at some point in each of their lives, every person in the audience had glimpsed an instant which, for reasons perhaps not fully apprehended,

was for them unforgettable — a solitary moment by the
desert or the sea in which nothing more significant than
stillness had happened, an exalted passage of literature or
music that had come suddenly and unexpectedly and was
never experienced in that way again, a sculpture on the
outside of an obscure building, a capable human hand seen
briefly in the coffeeshop: an instant when each had felt that
a different kind of existence was possible.

Each person in the audience had also at some point
wondered why the magical sense of living they'd often felt
when they were children had gone away — and where did it
go? And why was life so often ridden with anxiety? Why was
life so often dull, depressing, unfulfilling?

But on that sweltering Las Vegas night when they
watched Dusty May move and dance, and when they saw
her ankle snap and heard its concussive report, and when
they saw what she did after that, each and every one of them
knew that answers to those questions existed and that the
answers were real and true: because they each saw magnified in her this special sense of living they all at one time or
another had glimpsed.

A *fouetté* is a whipped turn when the dancer does a full
turn in pirouette, which is followed by a *plie* on the standing
leg, while the working leg extends and is whipped around to
the side and then, once extended to maximum turnout, bent
and pulled back in to a *passe* position behind the knee of the
supporting leg, which rises en pointe. The working leg is
always kept lifted and does not touch the ground.

When Dusty's ankle busted at the end of her dance, she
staggered but she did not fall. The shock came into her like
a poison dart, releasing a billion toxic organisms throughout
her body, the pain rolling through her in ceaseless waves.
The music mounted in climax and she took it in. She shut

her eyes. Then she lifted from the floor her broken leg and with her good leg performed fifteen full-turn pirouettes en pointe, whipping the broken leg so that it flopped sloppily. And, pulling it back and resting it behind the knee of her standing leg, Dusty May in this way finished a dance part gymnastics and part ballet.

53

THE CROWD DISSOLVED in pure pandemonium. She was still standing — almost hopping on the foot of her good leg — when a warm hand touched her left shoulder. She turned. She thought it was the announcer who'd given her the A-OK sign, but for a moment she wasn't sure. Yes, it's him, she thought. She was vaguely aware also that the entire arena had risen: they were giving her a standing ovation.

The applause was thunderous.

The announcer lifted her in his arms and carried her offstage. Her leg hung limp. Her dark skin was cotton-white, and for some time Dusty sincerely believed that death had singled her out.

"You're okay," the announcer whispered in her ear, as he carefully swept her offstage, "you're okay. You're amazing."

He kept repeating these words to her. His voice was quaking and breaking, and even in her half-delirious state, she thought he sounded as if he might come undone.

He took her into a sterile white room where a young sports medicine doctor was swinging one foot and waiting. Lightly, the announcer set her down. Waves of pain and nausea rolled continuously through her. The pain was enormous — like a living creature inside her. She felt herself unable to speak. She flailed once for a trashcan but missed. Then the trashcan was underneath her, and she began violently to vomit into it. She vomited until her stomach cramped, and for a long moment she couldn't take a breath.

"You're okay, you're okay."

She heard the announcer's calming voice and she felt his calming hand on her back, and then she realized that her faculty of awareness was slipping away. A moment later, she thought she again heard the announcer's voice, but it came to her as though from a great distance, and she did not understand that he was back onstage.

"Folks, in all my life I have never seen anything — *anything* — like that, and you've got to be astounded at what this incredible little girl stands for..."

The crowd exploded.

Dusty May went black.

54

WHEN SHE AWOKE, she was in the same room. The doctor was stabilizing her broken ankle with an air-cast. The nausea had diminished, but the pain had not. It came through her in deep sea currents and huge ocean rollers. She sat up. The doctor told her to go easy. She saw her ballet slippers on the floor. They'd been cut from her feet with scissors. They were shredded and soaked in her blood. She thought she perhaps also saw a human presence kneeling on the floor, but this made no sense. The livid light over her head lanced her eyes. She squished her eyes shut.

"You don't need to do that," the doctor said, but she didn't understand. She didn't know that he was not speaking to her.

She opened her eyes again. Her feet had been cleaned, and the bleeding in her toes had slowed. She saw herself in a flecked mirror across from her: her two Indian-black eyes and her silken black hair pulled tightly back and pinioned to her skull, her face sweat-streaked and drawn and pale still.

"You're going to be okay."

At first, she thought that it was the doctor or the announcer who said this, but then she realized it was not:

It was David genuflecting on the floor cleaning up her blood and very gently cleaning her mending feet. Her broken ankle was swollen to the size of a grapefruit, and horribly bruised. Then Dusty felt Sheila's warm hand grasp hers. Dusty gazed around and saw Sheila's calm wise face and David at her feet, and she knew then that she was safe.

AT AN ALL-NIGHT TRUCK stop on the edge of the desert, Dusty came in on crutches and exchanged a ten-dollar bill for a roll of quarters. A light rain was falling outside. Her thin dark arms were stippled with raindrops. She went to a payphone and rested her crutches against the wall and began punching quarters into the payphone slot. Then she dialed.

It was well after midnight, yet he picked up on the second ring. He did not speak. He did not breathe and he did not say anything. And then he started to ask something — no actual words, only a quick intake of breath — but abruptly he broke off. This was a grave miscalculation — and they both realized it at the same time. They both grasped the magnitude of his mistake.

"Who is this?" Kenneth Dvorak said on the other end of the phone, with another breath intake. But it was too late: some subtle quality in his voice rang untrue and fake.

"This?" Dusty said. "This is the bones you could not break."

KENNETH DVORAK HELD the phone to his ear for a long moment after the connection with Dusty had gone dead. He stared contemplatively at the white wall before him. When he hung up at last and turned around, he half expected to see her standing there, drenched in blood, with murder in her eyes.

But she was not there. He was totally alone in his home. And then, through the large window on his left, which gave to the huge western night, he saw the flash of horses in the pastures beyond — a flash of ghostly white.

He turned from the window. On a large table in his living room, he had set up an intricate reenactment of the battle of Waterloo, his interest in history deep and abiding. The army of soldiers on the table were lifeless little green men. He'd placed them strategically everywhere. On the other side of this table, standing mute against the wall, were three small porcelain dolls, epicene, vampiric, beautifully rendered, which he himself had sculpted.

Without apparent emotion or effort, Kenneth Dvorak strode over in his high boots to the dolls above whom, mounted on the wall, was the baseball bat Ted Williams had hit his last homerun with.

Dvorak had bought this bat years ago at an auction.

He took it down from the wall and with a mighty slugger's swing, he knocked the heads off all three of his porcelain dolls and then he smashed them to pieces.

He clubbed them.

After that, he smashed the little green army men and the table that comprised his intricate reenactment of Waterloo.

The whole violent outburst lasted less than two minutes, after which he went upstairs to Dusty's old bedroom. He stood upon the threshold and looked inside. The room was clean and illuminated brightly by moonlight and starlight coming in from outside. Her made bed was empty.

He gazed about the room for a long time, with thoughtful eyes.

He stared longest at a solitary photo of Dusty May that stood upon her little cherrywood desk which the two of them — Kenneth and Dusty — had built together. In the photo, her sharp-featured Lakota face and her dark eyes burned brightly, something coltish about her, he'd always thought, but they did not burn as brightly as her smile, the gap between her front teeth which he'd always found so ineffably endearing.

At last, he shut her door forever and went back downstairs.

He turned on music — a lachrymose piano nocturne of complicated harmonics, which stirred him deeply. He checked his old-fashioned pocketwatch. He realized only then that the watch had stopped. It had wound all the way down.

So it was now that he began winding the watch back up, winding and winding until it could go no more, and then he set the time accurately against his grandfather clock. He stared at the lunar glow of his pocketwatch and listened for a long moment to the rhythmic, insect-like tick coming from its intricate inner parts. The music all around him softly soared.

Then he shut out all the lights, and he danced alone.

He danced rhythmically and so nimble, his great bald pate floating moon-like through the room — dancing to the lovely soaring music, an enormous human, a marvel of motion, this mountainous man, alone over the shards and the wreckage of his delicate creations, moving in double-time now and so lightly through the dark corridors and many rooms of his gigantic mansion.

57

OUTSIDE THE RAIN HAD SLACKENED. The parking lot lay damp and deserted save for a solitary chrome-and-blue semi gleaming wetly under the gas-station lights. A soft wind whistled in from the west. She rested her crutches against the brick wall outside and sat down on a bench behind her. Her left leg pulsed in concert with her heartbeat. She closed her eyes and listened to the whistling wind. It had the smell of distance in it and rain and faraway grass. And freedom. She listened to the music of the wind for a very long time.

When she opened her eyes, she saw that there were green stars everywhere before her and meteors rocketing like fireworks across the western sky. She thought of the arcing firmament, and she remembered who had taught her that term, the long arc and architecture of the universe and its indestructible integrity, and the arc of her life as well, which was no less real and which had in many ways just begun.

She continued to sit. The dawn was approaching.

At length, she turned and watched the early morning light spread like milk across the entire eastern sky, a fleet of pewter clouds scudding in over the horizon like blimps and etched perfectly there, backlit by the coming sun. In a small quadrant of the north, just above a low range of hills, her eye caught a strange sector of dawn light. It was bluer than any other part of the sky — a self-contained pool of cornflower, with the peculiar pristine intensity of something viewed through the wrong end of binoculars. There it lay, beneath a cluster of creamy clouds, miniaturized and remote, yet exact in every detail, shrunk down fantastically but faultlessly rendered.

She watched it for a long time.

As she watched it, a waitress came outside from the truck-stop diner and asked Dusty if she was okay. The woman wore a turquoise bracelet and was white-haired and dark-skinned, Lakota. Her name tag was not fully visible but said Shonda.

"Yes," Dusty said. "I wanted to be alone."

The woman nodded once and smiled. She had a gap between her front teeth.

"You have a beautiful smile," Dusty said. She smiled in return.

"So do you."

The woman went back inside, and Dusty's foot pulsed more painfully still, and it occurred to her in the gaining light that perhaps he'd orchestrated the whole thing, but even if he had, she thought, he did not know what the outcome would be and could never have known, because the human will, as he had taught her also, is bottomless and unconquerable — "not even God can conquer it," he once said to her — and the will is free.

Just then, someone's warm and young muscular hand

touched her shoulder and passed to her a creased slip of paper.

She unfolded it.

It was a check made out to Dusty May, from the office of one Hollis D. Nickles, Esquire, and signed by Kenneth Dvorak, in the amount of fifty-thousand dollars.

She had won.

THE END

27998108R00117

Made in the USA
San Bernardino, CA
04 March 2019